Trauma, Traps, and Impermanant Tragedy:

A Hooligan's Guide to Saving the Kingdom

By Lily Olsen

For Sharla Means,
who always believed in my career as a writer, and
listened to my stories on the drive to soccer practice.

Chapter 1
The Piper

I remember the day I became the villain of your fairy tales.

It was the morning of the Summer Festival. The workers brought us all tins of water to rinse in. They were passed along the rows, so by the time one reached me it seemed more mud than water.

We'd been practicing for weeks to perform the play just right. All the pretty children, with golden hair and shining eyes, were dressed in white. They wore loaned jewelry around their wrists, necks, ankles, and even their ears. Tinsel was tied into their hair so they seemed to glitter with magick as they walked.

They were the ones that light seemed to follow, and the rest of us were in their shadow. We were the ones with ratty hair, scars on our faces and arms, twisted limbs, long noses, and birth splotches. We didn't get to wear white for the play, we wore the same clothes we always did. Dirty rags.

I remember sitting along the wall with the others as we

waited. The workers and volunteers were bustling around, and agitated dust swirled in the air. Framed by the aisles of beds was a girl at the end of the row. She had long hair the color of cream, and as the workers wove in tinsel she laughed. Light from the high windows landed on her, making it look like she was glowing.

They'd given her more food than her stomach could handle. She'd left half a roll on the vanity. My stomach growled as I looked at it.

We wouldn't be fed until after the show, or more accurately, during the show.

When everyone was ready the workers led us from the building in one long line to the square.

The pretty children were the heroes of the performance, saving the village from a plague of rats, singing and dancing and talking just to show how perfect they were. I had been cast as a wicked minstrel who tried to sneak rats into peoples homes. I only had a few lines, and got to play one horrible melody on a little penny whistle before I was thrown off stage by the pretty children.

The stage was built around the old gallows. I remember looking down; the rotted boards under my feet had long scratches. I stood right where they kicked the stool out from under criminals.

Anytime I said or did anything devious, the crowd threw rotting food at me. It was the first food I'd gotten that week, so I ignored the mold and the maggots.

I looked out during the final scene. The heroes were holding hands and singing like angels. Paper banners stretched over the streets, red and yellow to symbolize Summer. Booths at the edges of the square hawked all kinds of goods: some tantalizing scents carried all the way to where I was standing.

The crowd started clapping and cheering, and we all rushed on stage to take our bows. Then the harassed workers separated the children. The heroes were all ushered toward the crowd, to mingle and get interest. They were always adopted quickly, and the boy who played the King was always fought over.

I was just escorted back through the streets to the orphanage. Kids behind me in line picked chunks out of my hair and off the back of my shirt.

One of them scraped something off my shoulder, "you got lucky this year," they licked off their greedy fingers, "you've got chocolate."

That's what convinced me, I think. Someone calling me lucky.

I ducked out of line and started down an alley. The kids cried out, more because they hadn't gotten all the fruit than because they were worried about my escape. I could hear workers dashing my direction, so I started to run. I knew the workers would give up after a few blocks, one less mouth to feed and all.

The cobblestones were a blur under my feet, even after I came to a stop. Everything started to spin, and I fell against a brick wall. My head pounded as I looked up. The banners started spinning above my head, faster and faster. They seemed like a whirlpool about to swallow me up. I tried to stumble forward, but I tripped over my own feet and fell into a puddle of dirty water.

The penny whistle from the play rolled across the cobbles.

I groaned, and once the world stopped rotating, I flipped onto my back. People were passing on the thoroughfare beside me, but they paid me no heed.

The sun slowly melted behind the horizon, and people stopped passing my way.

I shuffled until I was sitting against a building. I was afraid that if I stood I'd black out.

My fingers and toes began to tingle with the cold, and my stomach seemed to be digesting itself. Pinpricks of white danced in my vision.

The whistle shone in the last ray of the dying sun. It seemed a magical thing, then. With the golden light glinting off it, it seemed to be made of precious metals.

I reached for it. You'll have to allow me this; in my starving delirious state, I felt that even touching a thing that appeared so cloaked in majesty, could fill my soul. Perhaps not my stomach, but it could fill the deeper hunger, some spiritual well could run over.

And in a way, I was right.

I lifted the whistle to my lips, and my hand was shaking so horribly I could barely hold it.

The metal was cold, cold enough it seemed to sear my skin. I breathed out and the resulting sound was the mournful call of a dying thing.

I closed my eyes and flexed my fingers.

The next sound was a melody, not the one I'd learned for the play, but one I'd learned from the actual village minstrel. It was a nursery rhyme about a drowned girl. In the story she sang the melodies of the wind, and the song sounded wild.

When I played through all I knew, I repeated it. Over and over and over, until the notes and their echoes danced ballet to the tragedy.

Somewhere, deep in my heart, I believed death was approaching. I kept playing until I could hardly breathe, because I felt that it would be better to die a minstrel than an unwanted child.

My fingers twitched up and down the instrument, sticking to the cold tin.

Then I was too cold and too hungry and paralytically afraid of death and the whistle fell from my mouth.

There was no light to turn the inside of my eyelids red. The cold had numbed my limbs. I'd starved before. I'd been frostbitten in cold attics with no blankets. I'd even lain beaten in alleys, unable to move. This time felt different.

Perhaps it was dramatic, but I let out a breath, and waited, fully expecting, the icy embrace of death.

Something pricked my side, something sharp and needlelike. I would've cried out, if I had any air.

The sensation continued, and a similar one began on my ankle. Soon the prickling sensation seemed to cover my entire body, but I knew it wasn't the feeling of a visitation of the grim reaper.

How did I know? Because accompanying the sharp piercing sensation was one of warmth. Warmth, and of fabric or fur against my bare skin.

My eyes opened to slits, and I peered through my eyelashes. Rats. Dozens, hundreds, thousands of rats were scrabbling across my skin, a roiling mass surrounding me.

I swallowed my heart and tried to move, to shake them off, to scream, to do anything.

My fingers twitched. The whistle still clutched in between them.

My lips parted, but no sound came out. The sudden image of a rat crawling into my mouth and down my throat came unbidden to my mind.

No. This wasn't the way I wanted to die.

I couldn't die this way.

The same thought that had haunted me before came back with an instinctive conviction.

Better to die a minstrel.

The whistle came up, the headjoint resting on my lip. A squeak of air forced its way out of my lungs, and a single note shattered the night.

Traveling parallel to that note was the command, get away.

I'd never have assumed they'd listen, but they did. They fell back leaving a semi-circle of rodent-free space around me.

My clothing was torn from their claws and they'd left muddy tracks across the fabric. Yet, there were no holes riddling my skin. No blood welled up from the tiny marks they'd left.

I breathed my amazement, and out came a song. A simple tune. My fingers moved without my conscious direction, and a sad little melody filled the air.

The rat's tails rose up, in an eerily familiar motion. They danced like the snakes charmed by shamans.

They began to scurry more frantically, racing back and forth, crawling over each other in frantic motion.

Some left, scrambling out of the alley and onto the moonlit streets.

Soon the rats were coming close to me, moving with strange reverence. They left things for me. Bread crusts, slices of fruit, one even managed a bowl of water.

If you recall, I was starving and delirious. I didn't even stop to think if it was safe to eat what the rats had given me. They were probably figments of my imagination anyways.

I swallowed the food, and it seemed to stick to my dry throat. The water was metallic but tasted like a miracle.

They didn't stop. They brought me meat scraps, beans, and even a few shining coins.

I ate off the ground like a dog.

By the time the sun sprouted from the horizon I was moving and more awake than I'd almost ever felt.

People screamed as they saw me in the dark, and soon a crowd had gathered.

I never explained that I could control the rats, but the people seemed to understand.

A tall man stepped to the forefront. His features were so distinguished that he had to be an aristocrat. Well, his features and the golden buttons on his suit.

A girl held his hand, tinsel still streaming in her hair.

She pointed at me, "he's from Saint Marthas!"

The aristocrat nodded, "Yes Anna, he probably is. What are you doing with these rats, boy?"

I shrugged.

Those of you who know my story probably know what's about to happen.

I, the piper, led every rat from our town out the front gate with nothing but a penny whistle. The aristocrat had promised I would be paid, and paid handsomely, for my efforts. I could live the life of a King.

When I returned to take my reward, the aristocrat sneered, his hooked nose wrinkling. He said he'd never actually give a poor pied piper anything. I was a devil worshiper, and apparently worse, I was a dirty, unwanted orphan boy.

He threatened to have me thrown in jail if I didn't leave. As soon as I stepped back, his maids hurried onto the front porch, as if my very presence had sullied it.

The girl who'd held his hand peeked at me through the window. She stuck out her tongue, then disappeared behind the curtains.

Unlike what happened with the rats, my whistling was intentional this time.

I made up the tune as I went, sticking to notes that sounded angry and harsh in my ears.

Here is the slight divergence from the traditional story. If you've heard of the Pied Piper, you probably have heard that I stole all the children from the city, and they were never seen again.

In reality, I stole the adults.

Every person over a year older than me followed me out onto the streets in a zombie parade. They shuffled into each other, tripped on the cobblestones, and kept their eyes aimed straight ahead. They ignored their kids as they tugged at their sleeves and asked questions in vain. When their scuffing feet almost drowned out my music, I played louder.

Chapter 2
Kennedy

We weren't the best thieves in the city, probably not even the best on the block, but no one could say we weren't determined. We did our jobs with reckless abandon, and the night we robbed the King was no different.

Either some semblance of intelligence or a miracle meant we were attempting to rob a supply wagon of the Kings and not the actual palace. Tanner would've been content with either, but as I planned to survive the operation, the wagon was a much better choice.

I suppose there's a question of why we had to rob the King in the first place. Most kids from the capital slums were pickpockets and burglars, and they did well enough. The problem was that Tanner and I had begun to develop a reputation in certain circles: a reputation of surviving difficult situations, of stealing priceless objects from the most brutal and greedy collectors. They kept our secrets, and gave us good prices, because they knew the payout would be generous. If we returned to begging and thieving on the main streets, they'd turn us in without a second thought– they had enough poor children giving them the average spoils.

The mercenaries accompanying the wagon were tired. Unseasonable rainstorms had left the dirt road a nightmare, and their trip had taken nearly a day longer than they'd anticipated. The men were ready to retire, and lucky for us, that meant they probably weren't super vigilant.

I watched from my tree with baited breath as the men neared our trap. They didn't have torches, the rain had soaked them and they were essentially useless. The warriors resorted instead to squinting around with angry expressions, like old men who lost their glasses. There was no way they'd notice the net, buried carefully under just the right amount of mud.

I'd made sure to place the net far enough to the side of the road that it wouldn't be disturbed by the passing wagon, and sure enough, the front wheels passed without a catch. I grabbed hold of the rope that would trigger my trap, and hoped my shaking hands wouldn't accidentally set it off.

When two of the mercenaries, the ones following just behind and to the left of the wagon, stepped into my net I pulled with all my strength.

The trap worked perfectly. The simple pulley system I'd rigged a few days ago functioned exactly as I'd hoped. The four corners of the net lifted in perfect sync, trapping the startled men inside as it heaved them up into the leafy canopy.

Things didn't go so smoothly on my end. I'd been

terrified of pulling too weakly and making the trap useless, so I'd overcompensated. I'd leaned into the rope, pulling with my strength and my weight. There was a little too much slack and I found myself falling backwards from the branch, swinging wildly and hanging onto the rope for dear life.

The shouts of the two trapped men caused an immediate panic at the wagon, the other mercenaries who'd been nearly dozing off jerked to attention, the majority running toward the confused voices.

They were so distracted by the sudden commotion that they didn't notice me whipping around in the woods. My grip on the rope faltered and I slipped, my palms burning as the course fibers bit into them. I caught hold again, gripping it with my hands, my knees, and my ankles. My tongue had turned leaden from fear, which was good. If it hadn't I definitely would've screamed and then Tanner and I would both be dead.

As it was, after a moment of sheer terror, I managed to suck in a weak breath. I looked up and found that I hadn't fallen half as far as I thought I had. I took another breath and started to climb the rope, hand over hand, trying as best I could to channel my inner monkey.

When I'd managed to drag myself back onto the branch, I looped up the rope and looked toward the trap. I wouldn't have needed a counterweight, but as I'd been an impromptu one, the soldiers were hanging much higher in the trees than I'd planned. I hoped they weren't too afraid of heights.

I then turned my attention toward my partner. Before I even

spotted him however, my eyes were caught by the mercenary still standing by the cart. He had to be a northerner, no one else could be so huge. He was ankle deep in mud and even so, he seemed two heads taller than any man I'd ever seen and twice as broad. He looked like he could pull both the wagon and the attached oxen all the way to the capital.

Tanner was doomed.

He had dropped onto the wagon, and the waterproof covering lay in a heap by his feet. He was crouched to avoid being seen, and was digging through a canvas bag. He knew as well as I did that the canvas bags were just full of grain.

The targets were the boxes or the chests. We knew from experience that the boxes contained high quality weapons and jewelry that were worth a lot in the right circles. The chests, which were much smaller and easier to handle, were filled with gold coins straight from where they were stamped in the west.

Tanner didn't seem to put much heed into the plan, or into practically. He completely ignored both the boxes and the chests, instead rooting through the bags of food. He closed the bag he'd been shuffling through and opened the next. What on earth was he looking for? The guards would be back any minute!

"Leave it and get out of there," I muttered quietly. I knew he wouldn't hear me, but I hoped my instructions would somehow carry psychically. No such luck.

The northerner was squelching his way toward the wagon bed. He walked like a child playing the floor is lava, holding his leg high until he found a place to step, then breaking his other foot from the mud. It might've looked comical, except that there was something so threatening about his expression and posture that the effect was completely lost.

I turned my attention away from my brainless compatriot– who was searching a sac of potatoes– to check on the men I'd hoisted into the tree tops. They had started to rotate lazily, and their companions were still trying to figure out how to get them down. They'd decided that it was a bear trap and not a sudden attack, but that didn't exactly help them lower their friends.

"Cut the net," the scraggly one suggested.

"And fall three hundred feet to our deaths?"

I scoffed. They weren't nearly that high. At most they'd break their legs. If they were careful they'd only get a few bruises.

One of the hanging men had turned and was facing the wagon. Facing Tanner. An anxious energy infused him and he wiggled this way and that in the net.

"Wait! Benny, Tom, Ansel, look!" He stuck his hand through the net to gesture, but I didn't give him the opportunity. Tanner probably couldn't take on the northerner, but he definitely couldn't take on the northerner and the rest of them.

I tugged a release line, and the net dropped quickly. When the sudden descent stopped abruptly the men's heads banged together with impressive force. They both went limp.

Satisfied that I'd done my duty there, I turned back to see if Tanner had yet to stop fiddling with the grain.

As a matter of fact he had. A small chest was tucked in the crook of his elbow, and I felt a rush of elation. He had it! We could take it and lose the warriors in the woods!

Except of course, we couldn't. The northerner had just high stepped to the back of the wagon. He didn't draw his sword, but it wasn't because he was going to show mercy. He simply didn't need it.

"Help! Thief!" He bellowed, the powerful sound scaring the birds nesting in nearby trees to take to the air in panic.

A family of crows pummeled me in their tumultuous exodus, one sickly bird smacking me right in the face.

I didn't have any space to stumble back, but it wasn't exactly a choice. And I didn't have a rope this time. Jolly.

I plummeted out of the tree, spitting black feathers out of my mouth. Twigs and branches beat against my back as I fell, and try as I might I couldn't rotate enough to see the ground, let alone brace to hit it.

I landed flat on my back, my head slamming against the ground. All the air was forced from my lungs in a sudden torrent, and my bones vibrated in my skin. I couldn't move a muscle. I tried to imagine a swarm of little black dots darkening my vision, but I couldn't force myself to black out. I just had to lay there in the dirt, branches and rocks poking into my back, and some viscous liquid from the collision with the sickly bird dripping down my face.

Tanner was probably trying to take out the mercenaries with moves he'd learned from the local theater. As far as I knew, he had no actual understanding of any martial arts, and liked the flashy moves the actors and actresses used anyway.

He was also probably losing. Horribly. I hoped they'd kill him, instead of taking him prisoner or something. If he had any wits at all he ought to make them kill him, but his earlier betrayal to the plan didn't fill me with much trust.

I strained to hear what was happening, but the ringing in my ears was too loud. I don't know how long I lay there paralyzed, but it felt like forever. Actually it felt like more than forever. It felt like several eternities all thrown together and cooked up into a nasty stew of anticipation, anger, and mild panic.

When I finally could move I sat up slowly. It would be a shame to pass out now. My back hurt a lot, figures. There was a scrape on my shoulder that was bleeding, but it wasn't too bad. My arms were covered in nicks and scrapes, but that seemed the worst of it. Besides the blinding headache I mean. Everytime I took a step it felt like someone was taking a sledgehammer to my skull. No, not a sledgehammer…an anvil.

Tanner was probably slumped in some hasty grave though, so I couldn't quite complain.

I made my way to the road cautiously, in case the mercenaries were still there. They'd cleared out. No one was visible on the muddy road. They'd even somehow contrived to get the trapped ones out of the net. It hung limp and dangling. They must've sliced through. Maybe the ones below had tried to catch them.

I smiled picturing them waddling out of here with bruised backsides. Then I realized I was waddling too and stopped smiling.

It didn't take long to find Tanner.

I'd assumed they'd toss him aside after he'd died. If they were scared of repercussions they'd have dumped him in a shallow grave. Having been raised on stories of northerner brutality I'd even feared they may have taken his bones as trophies, which would've been a pain to collect.

They'd done none of those things. They'd made their ox trample him. I suppose to make it look like an accident or something. He was face up in the mud, hoof prints all across his clothing. His neck had been broken, probably the result of an aggressive backhand by the northerner. There was a clean split in his middle too, where he'd been run through by a long sword.

To cover these signs they'd filled the cavity the knife had left with mud, and his neck had been crushed under the wagon wheel. If I wasn't so familiar with the dead I might not have realized anything had even been staged.

I pulled my friend from the mud and laid him out on a mossy patch of earth. The effort sent twinges up my back but I could deal with it.

I arranged his limbs with precision, making sure the breaks in his bones lined up so they'd heal straight. I scooped some of the mud out of his chest before I decided it was too disgusting and eerie and I couldn't do it. It would probably purge anyway.

When everything was neatly laid out I sat beside my best friend's body.

Most people see necromancy as a bloody affair. The local bard claimed a necromancer had to pull out a man's heart, and give it a kiss, to reanimate a body. Parents scared their children into behaving with tales of necromancers who stole children and poured their blood into the mouths of the gaping dead.

Necromancy is much more like healing, albeit belated healing. Bones snap and click together, disease and sickness vanish, skin grows new and glowing, organs mend, nerves come unknotted, and the mind forgets the tragedy.

Watching it happen though, I suppose I can see where they get their stories. Until the bones and muscles have reiterated themselves they can be seen rippling under the skin like rodents. The skin must rot before it regenerates, and it comes off like old paint.

I don't have to mentally orchestrate the entire dance, which is good because I'd probably end up combining his spleen and stomach. I do have to start the process, spark it. I just need a little skin to skin contact and I can share my life.

Tanner opened his eyes and looked at me kneeling over him.

The work magick had wrought on him was very exact and fantastic, but he had still been a corpse. He couldn't move too quickly or the memories of rigor mortis would break his bones.

"You couldn't have caught the northerner in the net?" Tanner's voice wasn't raspy. His vocal chords were the healthiest they'd been since his last revival.

I shrugged, "Didn't see him."

Tanner turned his head to give me a look, "You're kidding right? He was the size of a mountain."

"Fine maybe I saw him but, I mean, I thought he was an ox!"

Tanner laughed incredulously.

"I'm not joking! He walked all hunched over and he's certainly got the muscles for it!"

"I think you need to get your eyes checked Edy," He pushed himself onto his elbows.

I stood up and held out a hand, "I've told you not to call me that light bringer."

Tanner ignored my hand and hopped up, "I was five. You can't hold that over me forever."

"Watch me. When you die for real I'm going to make sure it's on your grave."

"If I'm dead for real then you'd have to be dead."

"Or just hate you," I grin, "Keep calling me Edy and it might happen."

"I can't call you Kennedy. It's like twenty syllables."

I move back toward the road and my trap. I wanted to take it apart and bring the pieces home. I'd need a new net, but other than that, I could probably set this up again.

"What were you doing with the grain sacks?" I asked, beginning to clamber up the main tree of my contraption.

"Joey said nobles hide their enchanted things in them. I guess it's so thieves like us won't find them."

"Well obviously it didn't work all that well. Besides, we don't need enchantments Tanner. We need money," I tried to keep the edge from my voice. Tanner had an obsession with rare things. Things he either shouldn't have or that were one of a kind. He'd never even let me see his collection.

"These kinds of things are worth quite a lot."

At his words I looked down and found him rolling something between his fingers.

"So you got something? I'm impressed." I deadpanned.

"It's a ring. Supposed to enhance my strength or something"

"I'd bet you ten silvers I can still beat you in an arm wrestle."

Tanner, ever the showman, flexed, "I've been wrestling in the square. I've even won a few times."

"Against who? Ten year olds?"

"I beat a member of Befreiung der Verdammten once," Tanner blustered.

"That doesn't mean anything! I've met a five year old in that cult! They aren't particularly powerful."

Tanner made a dismissive gesture, "I'll bet *you* ten silvers I can still beat you."

"You don't have any silvers."

"I'm not planning to lose," He grinned.

I snorted and tugged the last piece of rope from the trees then I hopped down. I landed hard and a shock of pain ran along my injured back.

Tanner didn't notice. He was too busy stretching ostentatiously.

"Let's get home, then we can wrestle," I suggested. Tanner shrugged and we started down the muddy trail.

"We never came up with a good nickname," Tanner began, "What about–"

"No."

"But—"

"No."

When we got closer to the city wall Tanner tucked the strength ring into his boot. He wasn't inconspicuous, all covered in cloven hoofprints and with hair that seemed to be a solid brick of mud. Still, we weren't from the wealthiest part of town. The flashes of silver from that ring would send the message that we were worth robbing.

"Mum wants to have you over for dinner," Tanner said, "she's even planning to make that disgusting vegetable soup you like."

Tanner's mum was a master with soups and her vegetable stew was to die for. Her breads were good too, as long as I didn't feel too attached to my teeth.

"Arm wrestle then?" I asked.

Tanner nodded, "Don't forget your silvers."

Chapter 3
Kennedy

I had just put away the ropes when someone pounded on the door.

"I'll get it!" my sisters said at the same time. They raced past my doorway and a loud thump implied they'd run into the door.

I snagged a pouch of silvers from my desk and peeked around the doorframe.

My blood froze in my veins. My sisters had opened the front door and a single man filled the entire opening.

"Are your parents home?" the northerner asked. His voice was big, and it echoed through the house hollowly.

My sisters split up to ask both Mom and Dad. They shouldn't have bothered with the second, but they held onto the hope that he'd leave the house at some point.

I withdrew my head and pressed my back against the wall. He had to be here for me. Why else would he show up here? Had they spotted me in the woods? Even then how did they know where I lived?

My moms footsteps hurried toward the front door.

"Can I help you?" she asked, and I knew from her tone she was holding onto the door, ready to shut it in the man's face if he didn't have something good to say.

"Do you have a Kennedy in your house?"

"Who's asking?"

"Servants of the King." His voice was so loud the art on the walls shook and trembled at the sound.

"Go get your sister will you," Mom asks quietly.

She waits until my sisters are walking to come get me before addressing the man again, "Whatever happened I'm sure we can sort it out here, right? No need for the King?" There was so much worry in her tone that my own nearly tripled.

My sisters stepped into my room at the same time.

"Kennedy Mom needs you!"

I tucked the pouch of silvers back into the desk, and followed them out into the hall before they began an impromptu game of tag and ran off.

Mom was indeed standing in the doorway, one hand on the door knob. She was wearing her old checkered apron, and it was dusted with a good helping of flour. Globs of dough clung to her fingertips, and there was a streak of it on her forehead.

I turned my attention away from her to look at the northerner.

The man had stepped back from the door and didn't seem to fill it in the same enormous way as before. He looked less like a warrior and more like a misplaced stable hand.

"What is it Mom?" I kept my voice as steady and unconcerned as I could.

"This gentleman is here on behalf of the King. I think he wanted a word with you."

She gave me the signature, 'on your best behavior' look.

I stepped up and pretended not to recognize the man, "What does his highness need me for?"

The northerner looked decidedly out of place when he said, "The King, er, his highness, needs to speak with you."

That made it sound like he was a concerned parent.

"When does he request this audience?" I clenched my fist in my pocket. None of the guards had seen me, but other than this job what would I be needed for? Lord Donnovan couldn't be behind this, he'd fallen out of favor with the king.

My mind was racing. Had I left any identifiers on the net? Was my name somewhere on my equipment? Then something much scarier hit me. Tanner. He was the only way they could've found me. Had they caught him alive again? How'd they force him to give up my name?

"Right now," the mercenary stepped off the stoop and started walking up the street, obviously intending me to follow.

"Shouldn't I at least change into something more formal?" I could grab a lock pick kit, in case I got thrown into a dungeon or something.

The northern paused, "He didn't say. Let's just go."

I glanced at my mom with my patented, 'wish me luck' look.

She bit her lip and closed the door behind me.

Not far down the street one of the King's steam powered trolleys was puffing. The northerner stepped in and offered a hand to help me up.

I ignored him and climbed in on my own. The bronze exterior was well kept, although mud from recent travels splattered the bottom of the carriage. The interior as well was made of bronze, and the benches were cold to the touch. Steam poured from several pipes sticking from the back.

The driver pulled a lever and the wheels began to roll.

If I hadn't been so drunk on adrenaline I probably would've focused more on discovering how exactly it worked. I'd tried to make steam powered traps before, but none of my attempts had been very effective.

"If you don't mind me asking, why does the King want to talk to me?" I asked, trying to sound nonchalant.

The northerner hadn't struck me as a very diplomatic man, and it turned out I had read him right.

He shrugged, "Something to do with a walking deadman and a problem in the east."

There were only two options for the walking deadman part, and one of them was safely at home. This had to be about Tanner. How had they found him? He was normally so cautious on his way home.

I racked my brains for any news about problems in the east. All I could recall were the usual higgledy-piggledy rumors about bad crop, and rising potato prices. There was also a comment

Ginger had made about her mother's connections going dark, but I doubted that had anything to do with it.

Unless….there could be some kind of disease or famine in the east. Maybe the King was trying to find me because he was collecting necromancers to send to raise the dead. No, that was too dramatic. Everything was probably fine. Maybe the northerner had misheard.

I couldn't help but imagine standing in some dirty medicine hut in the east, rows of dead bodies lined up around me. I shook the image from my head and the northerner gave me a strange look.

The trolley moved much more smoothly than the horse drawn carts I'd been in before, although I couldn't help but notice that it didn't turn quite as easily.

It took us through familiar alleys, and then into the richer part of town. We started passing other mechanical carts on the roads, and buildings still lit despite the hour.

Joey's house was among them, and a firelight glowed through the elegant windows. Fancy men and women in layers of impractical clothing were laughing as they spilled out the front doors. Joey always said his parents hosted too many parties.

The palace loomed closer and closer, and I was hit again with a rush of gratitude that I hadn't chosen to rob it. Even the back entrance was intimidating. The gate towered fifteen feet high, the walls were lousy with holes for archers to fire out of, and there were nigh a dozen men in full armor standing to either side of the gate.

26

Two of them stepped up to stop the carriage. The northerner jerked a lever and the cart jolted to a stop.

"Name and business," one of them asked, his voice muffled by the face guard.

"Yith Hassyet, by the King's request," the northerner mumbled, searching his pockets until he found the official writ of passage.

The guards offered hands to help us down. I ignored mine, but the northerner took the man's hand. The man nearly collapsed from the weight.

We were escorted through the gate and into the well manicured interior.

The defenses were even more intimidating from inside. Guards jogged through the pathways, clutching the leashes of dogs twice my size. A strange latticework of pipes lined the castle wall, no doubt intricate traps created to stab, throw, or otherwise maim any intruders.

"The King must feel pretty safe inside all this," I comment.

The northerner grunts, "Pretty sure he has it cause he doesn't feel safe."

Fair enough.

The guards jostled us up to a door. A harassed looking woman let us in and led us up several flights of stairs.

Did I say several? I mean millions. There were so many wretched stairs my thighs were burning by the time I reached the King's floor, and I'm in shape!

The northerner was struggling too. He panted as he walked,

and leaned heavily on the railing.

The serving woman didn't seem to notice the abundance of stairs. She sped up them without the slightest pause, and waited for us at the top.

Once we caught up and caught our breath she tucked a lock of my hair behind my ear, and pulled open a set of ridiculous iron doors.

I'd heard stories of the elegance of the King's Throne Room. This obviously wasn't it.

There were no loft ceilings or marble pillars. Instead there were stone walls adorned only with torches. There was a red carpet lined with gold, and fancifully carved armchairs lining the walls. It seemed like a meeting room, but there was no table. Instead there was a single standing desk, which the King stood behind.

If the room had been a shock, the King was doubly so. He looked like any other man, almost no distinguishing features whatsoever. His hair was marked with silver lines of age, his nose was slightly crooked. His lips were drawn into a tight line, and the whole of his face seemed bent toward it.

The woman cleared her throat, "The Necromancer, sir."

So they knew. A cold terror ran down my spine like an icy finger.

The Northerner cleared his throat, as if expecting his own introduction.

The King didn't look up from whatever papers held his attention.

"Leave us, Marie. Take the giant with you."

28

The woman glanced at me before she left. Something in her expression seemed almost maternal, then she turned away and pulled the Northerner behind her.

The iron doors closed with a bang that echoed through the chambers.

The King looked up. There had been no remarkable features on his face before, but his eyes changed his entire appearance. They were hazel, and they seemed to emanate a fierce glow that accentuated his cheekbones. The gray in his beard turned to silver. His somewhat crooked nose gained some kind of majesty.

The effect was quite incredible. His exactly-regular face had become something imposing. This was a man no one would dare cross.

"Do you consider yourself foolish?' His voice matched his eyes, domineering and powerful.

"No, sir. Sire. Your highness?" How was I supposed to address the King? I'd never been taught the etiquette. I suppose he could add it to the list of reasons I could be hanged.

First, robbing his wagon, although they may still consider it just an attempted robbery. Second, necromancy of a criminal. Third, calling him the wrong title. Legally, I could be labeled a traitor for any one of them. Together, it didn't look great for me.

"I appreciate your confidence. It's an important trait," the King took a step away from the desk, "but perhaps confidence has a tendency to lead to foolhardiness."

I nodded. I knew he'd just insulted me, but he was a King for heaven's sakes. What was I supposed to say?

"The ancients said all traits are on a spectrum. Confidence is a balance between cowardice and foolhardiness." The King looked at his feet, and in the absence of his gaze I felt myself able to breathe again.

Should I try to run? Did I have any hope of escape?

He looked back up, "Your partner seems much more foolhardy than you. He walked right into the path of the soldiers he'd robbed. He seemed to think he could fight them all at once."

He must've been testing the ring.

"Of course they subdued him quickly, my men are the best. My alchemists are equally high achievers, and the truth serum worked a charm...I digress."

The quality of his tone had changed, and he seemed more professorial than noble.

"Have you heard of the troubles in the east?"

"Only rumors, your highness."

His eyes sharped, "What rumors?"

"Uh, dark things. People losing correspondence, bad crop..."

The King relaxed a little, "I see. There are indeed dark things in the East."

"Are you planning to send me there? Sire?" It would be better than being hanged, that was for sure.

"Yes, I am. There is a terror threatening that part of the kingdom. A piper."

I waited for the rest. The King just stood there staring at his toes. He was reduced to a normal man for those seconds, his stature and expression falling back to an unglorified average.

"I don't think I heard you right, sir. Did you say a piper? Like a musician."

He didn't look up, "No, you heard me correctly. They call him the pied piper. He's been taking men and women from their homes. They say he's making an army."

An army? I couldn't fight an army. Unless they'd already caused so much devastation that I was needed to revive them. Was I being sent with the King's soldiers? To heal them if they fell?

"So he's a revolutionary?"

The King looked up, his face a combination of rage and terror.

"No!" His bellow echoed off the walls, "He is a rebel. He is taking the minds of innocent civilians and bending them to his will. He is a criminal, a witch. He must be stopped."

I took a step back, pushed by the force of his words.

"Shouldn't you send an army then? Stop his before it's–"

"No, we cannot send an army. They'd fall under his spell. This is why we need you. Children have fled in flocks from the Eastern provinces, they're the only ones immune to his magicks. Naturally teenagers are the oldest children," the King began to pace, "so we need a party of them willing and capable of taking down this Pied Piper. The problem is that I will be penalized for anything that happens during the attack, and teenagers are bound to make stupid decisions and die," the King turned to me, "You will be there to keep them alive."

I pride myself on being clever. I may be illiterate, and I may have never been to school, but I was smart. I designed traps, I understood concepts easily, and I could beat anyone at a game of Tricks.

And I was completely clueless. Utterly lost.

"My General will help you gather a team."

There was a sound like honeybees trapped in my ears. My thoughts were stuck in syrup, sticky trails of molasses pulling at the letters as they tried to arrange themselves.

Everything seemed to hit me at once. There was a witchard in the east, and I was being sent to stop him. He had an army. I was being sent to stop him. The King needed me to stop a rampaging wicked witchard who enchanted people and had an army and I was being sent with a group of teenagers.

"What?"

The King ignored my squawk, stepping back around his desk and continuing to look at his papers. He shuffled them around a little bit, then pulled out a yellowed page.

He held it out to me. When I didn't move he looked up and swirled it through the air to catch my attention.

"Take it."

I did.

The King called for the maid. The door was open before he finished his sentence.

The maid bustled in, and gripped my shoulders. She must've had practice at dealing with people in shock, because she guides me out of the room with expert poise. Once the door is closed behind us, she spins me around.

"Your friend is already with the general, I assume I'm

suppoed to escort you there as well?

I looked down at the paper clutched in my fingers.

"Yep. That's what it looks like."

Once again the woman's expression melted from stern to something motherly.

"They don't plan to hang you dear, or you would've been sent to the gallows and not the General."

She sounded so optimistic, I nearly fell for it. But no, my occasional pessimism would take the day. The King's plan (which didn't even qualify as a plan) was to send a bunch of teenagers to stop a magician, and a teenage necromancer to keep them alive. The main problem, ignoring the whole stop an evil magician part, is that I was a stupid teenager too, and if I died no one could revive me.

I nodded, and let the woman guide me through the complex corridors and pathways. At one point she pulled aside a tapestry to reveal a door.

"Short cut."

Luckily, we only had to climb a few stairs before we reached the Generals chambers.

They weren't nearly as richly decorated as the King's chambers. There was a desk, but it was scuffed and stained by ink. Stacks of papers rustled from the breeze of the open window. There were three mugs on the corners of his desk, each with a line of steam rising from them. A suit of armor was against the far wall, and there was an arrangement of three simple chairs in front of the desk.

The General stood up as we entered, "Thank you Marie," his eyes flicked to me, "It's Kennedy right?"

He was tall, and well built. His brown hair was cropped short, his beard shaved to stubble. His eyes were hooded, and his eyebrows thick. His jaw was square in a way that put me in mind of a farmer. He looked, well, simple.

"Right. Are you the General?" I asked.

The woman whispered that I should hand him the paper. I'd almost forgotten I had it.

"Please, have a seat," he smiled, more out of obligation than joy, "Marie, could you get Tanner for me?"

Marie nodded, and left the room with soft footsteps.

I sat on one of the wooden chairs.

"You already visited the King, I see," he looked at the paper I'd handed him.

"Knowing him, he probably didn't explain very well."

"Not very well, no," I replied. Then my stomach dropped. Was it treasonous to speak ill of the King? Did that count as speaking ill? The general had done it first so it was probably fine, right?

"There's a man in the Eastern part of the Kingdom. The reports say he's taken control of all the adults in Kartoffelstadt, with nothing but the sound of his flute."

The General had a distracted air, like his mind was full of names, dates, and facts that all vied for his attention. When he lapsed into silence it seemed as if it was because he'd forgotten I existed, and not because there was nothing else to say.

"Is that why potatoes are so expensive right now?" I wasn't really curious, I just wanted to remind him, politely, that I was there.

He took a sip from the first of the three mugs, and winced when he swallowed.

"Yes, yes, it has caused some trouble. They haven't been shipping their produce as usual…"

This time I let him stare into the distance for a good minute before I interrupted his thoughts.

"I'm sorry, were you going to explain what you plan to have me do?"

He blinked and his eyes cleared.

"Yes, I'm sorry. I've been a little under the weather recently," he paused, "the children weren't super descriptive, so we don't know everything about the case. As it happens we know very little about him, except that the adults obey him and the children are immune. I tried to send scouting parties but the King was having none of it. You'll be going in blind."

I wanted to ask questions, but didn't want to sound ignorant.

Marie stepped through the doors, tugging on a rope.

Tanner jerked into the room. The rope was tied around his chest. Thin cords held his wrists together, and someone had taken his boots.

And he was grinning. Smiling like a maniac.

"Hey Edy. Turns out they don't want to hang us just yet!"

Marie cleared her throat punitively, but the general just smiled.

"Nice to see you again Tanner. How was prison?"

"It was a short stay, thanks to your quick work," Tanner plopped down in the chair beside me, wincing as the rope tightened around his chest. Marie was jerked slightly forward.

"Thank you for escorting him Marie, we would like to talk in private if possible."

Marie said something back, but I leaned over and whispered to Tanner.

"Did you really go back and try to beat up the guards?"

He chuckled, "That would've been epic, but no. They ran into my on my way to Joey's."

"Why were you headed to Joey's? We already–"

I didn't finish my statement because Marie and the General had stopped talking. Marie bowed sardonically, and left.

The general turned to us, "I realized I neglected introductions. I'm George Kingsman," he offered his hand.

Tanner took it first, giving a firm handshake.

"Now for the deal. Both of you have committed high crimes, and we could sentence you to death, or servitude until *permenant* death," he gave us a sharp look, "The King and I would both prefer you to take this mission. If you were to succeed, you'd receive a full pardon."

Tanner was tipping back in his chair, the rope tied around his chest dragging on the floor. He didn't seem at all confused by what the mission was, so I assumed he'd already been briefed.

"Is it just me and Edy then?"

"Don't call me Edy," I growled under my breath.

"Ideally no. Unfortunately, we only keep records of adults, so we don't have anyone in mind. We'd give you a day to pick out other members of your party. If they don't pass the physical, they'll stay here."

"What if Edy here doesn't pass?"

I caught the trailing rope under my foot and dragged it. Tanner grunted as it tightened.

"Stop calling me Edy."

"She's necessary. If you don't pass however, you'll be sent to work in the stables."

"Don't worry about me. I'm incredibly fit," Tanner flexed his arms.

A sarcastic comment rose to my tongue, but I swallowed it down. I did want him to come, I couldn't point out his weaknesses in front of Kingsman.

"We'll see," Kingsman shuffled his papers, "the King will also do his own test of some kind to determine if you have the skills to continue. We don't want you to carry too much dead weight."

"Edy is good with dead weight," Tanner said. I knew he was using my nickname just to annoy me, because he stared right at me when he said it.

I kicked his chair.

The precarious balance he'd maintained lapsed. He tipped back, and his hands went out to stop his fall. They were still tied together, and he failed to catch hold of anything. His head hit the plush carpet with a thump.

Kingsman looked over his desk with an expression of vague interest, taking a sip of his drink.

"Are you ok down there?"

Tanner glared at me, "Just dandy. Can someone help me up?"

I shrugged, "If you say please."

Tanner rolled his eyes but did as I'd asked.

I knelt down at the back to help lift it, and Tanner whispered quietly enough Kingsman wouldn't hear.

"I was building an image there! He has to think I'm impressive or I won't be going!"

"Impressive and arrogant are two different things. My name isn't Edy."

As soon as Tanner was up, he tipped onto the back two legs again.

"George Kingsman," he began, with all the puffed-up dignity of a spoiled child, "someone is trying to have you poisoned."

Kingsman's eyebrows knit together, and he leaned back, "What makes you say that?"

"That mug," Tanner gestured with both his hands at the desk, "the steam is yellow-ish. Besides I'm familiar with a lot of poisons, and the air reeks of it."

Kingsman leaned forward again and peered into the cup. I stared too, and managed to catch the yellow tint to the steam as it rose.

"It is a different shade than my normal roast..." He pulled over the other two mugs to compare.

"I'm not entirely sure who it was that tried to have you killed, but if you finish that cup, you're dead meat," Tanner sounded extraordinarily proud of himself. He'd been beaten, killed, revived, beaten again, and imprisoned all in the space of a few hours. How was he so perfectly content? Why in heaven's name was he grinning like he owned the world?

"I don't know who'd want to kill you, probably a political rival. I doubt it was sent by the Piper already. Although I suppose we don't really know enough about him. He may have people here in the castle already. I'd suggest you double or triple your own defenses, and of course the King's," Tanner's voice was scratchy, they probably hadn't offered him much water in the cell, and coming back from the dead always left a person thirsty.

"I know how to defend myself," Kingsman seemed very entertained by the thought of having guards.

"Yes, but apparently not against poisons. Maybe a well informed attendant would do well."

"Are you offering?"

Tanner shook his head, "Nope, I'm going on the mission to make sure your precious necromancer here doesn't die. Like you said, she's necessary."

I felt a thrill at his last words. It wasn't because they were particularly flattering, quite the opposite in fact, but because it was such a good play. If he set himself up as the protector he wouldn't have to prove particular skill in anything. Based on the way George Kingsman was considering his mugs, he believed Tanner.

"I'd assume, if it was anyone, that it was probably the King.

I haven't met him, but the state of the dungeon and the abundance
of guards implies paranoia. Especially given just how many traps
we had to avoid to get here," Tanner coughed, his throat was
beginning to rasp.

"You're a pretty competent political rival, the people adore
you, the nobles respect you. You're a threat to the King, and he,"
Tanner grabbed one of Kingsman's mugs, "doesn't seem like a
man to tolerate threats." Tanner upended the glass, and took a
swallow.

Kingsman and I both stared, open mouthed.

"Tanner, that was the poison," I gape.

Tanner blinked, and swallowed hard. When he spoke his
voice was the sound of sandpaper, "I got that, thanks."

He tipped forward on his chair, resting it on all four legs. His
face became taut with pain, but he did his best not to show it. His
fingers gripped the armrests, his knuckles turning white. He began
to convulse, his entire body racked with powerful spasms.

"Tanner!"

I reached out to offer some kind of comfort, but Kingsman
held out a hand to stop me.

"Wait, I want to see you bring him back." Kingsman looked
at Tanner and winced. He stared at the wall, trying immensely hard
not to look at the dying boy across from him.

"I assume this is the teenage stupidity you were worried
about," I said. I didn't really care about the words, I just didn't
want to hear Tanner's groaning.

I knew he was in pain, probably a lot of it. My only comfort was that as part of the revival process, he would forget the mental trauma of the death. The pain would only last a minute. Unless the poison was slow acting, which I supposed it very well could be.

"Yes, this was the exact thing the King didn't want to cause big issues. Speaking of issues, you aren't allowed to tell anyone what you're doing. Your family will be told you're working off a charge of petty crime in the palace kitchens."

"That makes sense."

We were both talking loudly, trying to drown out Tanner's agony. Of course it didn't really work. His agony beat a familiar path in my heart.

"We don't want anyone finding out we have a genuine necromancer. We'd have a riot on our hands."

"I think I've decided who we need to–" Tanner passed out, "who we need to invite to join us," I finished.

"What're their names?" Kingsman tugged a piece of parchment from a stack, and readied his pen.

"Ginger Becker, she lives near Wide River."

"What are her abilities?"

"She knows the woods and wilderness well, and she knows what food would be edible. She's also a master at healing salves." I didn't mention that her mother was a witch, but that was a big part of it. Ginger and I had made dozens of potions over the years.

"We'll invite her here. Anyone else?"

"Joey Marcus. He's a noble."

"What does he do?"

I looked down, "he can read."

"Read? Do you mean maps?"

"No, I mean he's literate. He's educated."

My voice was small. I hated how it sounded, like the squeak of a mouse.

Kingsman must've sensed my shame, but he pretended not to notice, "I see…is there anyone else?"

"Not that I can think of. Tanner may have some suggestions."

Kingsman let his gaze stray to Tanner's limp body.

"Is he breathing?"

I looked across at him. Tanner is folded over, but he's not yet dead. I could see the life in him, booming dimly from his chest.

"Yes. He'll be dead soon though."

Kingsman hesitated, "How many times have you brought people back?"

"Six. Six times." Every single one was tattooed on my cranium.

"And there's no limit to your ability? I mean, we've been working under the assumption that there won't be."

I shook my head, "No limits as far as I've noticed. Oh, I suppose there have been seven. I can bring animals back from the dead too."

Kingsman leaned over the desk, and there was a curiosity that lit his eyes like the Kings.

"How dead is too dead to revive?"

"I don't know if there is a 'too dead'. I have to arrange the body so it comes back naturally, so maybe if it was…missing lots of parts.”

Tanner stirred, his spine arching. When he fell back I knew the life had left him.

“I can show you now, if you’d like.”

Kingsman nodded, and stood up. As I arranged the body on the ground Kingsman came around his desk and watched avidly.

Blood had dripped down Tanner’s chin, and I wiped it away with my sleeve.

“I have to make sure none of his limbs are bent out of place or it doesn’t all come together properly.

I then knelt beside his body, and brushed Tanner’s cheek with my fingers.

I saw the change begin immediately.

Kingsman leaned over, his attention rapt. I had no doubt he would record his observations later, and they’d disappear into his endless stack of papers.

Tanner’s eyes peeled open, and he sighed softly.

“I think I proved my point, George.”

Kingsman nodded, a distant look in his eyes, and went to help Tanner up.

“You have to wait a minute for the rigor mortis to go away,” I offered.

Kingsman hummed speculatively, “But rigor mortis oughtn’t to set in until at least 120 minutes after death. He was barely dead 3!”

I shrugged, “I don’t make the rules.”

To be fair, I didn’t even understand them.

Kingsman quickly stepped back to his desk and jotted something down on the corner of a page.

I waited until Tanner was ready to stand and offered my hand to help him up. I didn't expect him to take it. Every time I'd revive him, he'd ignored it and hopped up, as if to prove he was back to normal.

Always full of surprises, he took my outstretched hand.

He was shakier than I'd ever seen before, but he grinned like everything was going as normal.

"So, Mr. Kingsman, can we be off?"

He responded without looking up, "Off to where? You'll be sleeping here."

"In the palace?" I said, at the same time Tanner said, "you better be providing food too."

Chapter 3
Kennedy

Turns out our rooms were none other than private cells in the palace prison.

I should've expected it, given that we were criminals, but I'd been imagining beds with mattresses five hands tall, and overflowing with pillows. I'd imagined sheets made of silk and all the other materials I'd only ever heard off.

I got a dirty cobblestone floor, three walls of iron bars, a bed of straw, a bucket as a bathroom, and a murderer for a next-door-neighbor.

The only redeeming quality was that I was right next to Tanner.

We leaned against the back walls, resting our heads against the bars. It wasn't the first time we'd been thrown in jail, but normally they were the low-security overnight-stay kinds of prisons. This one had guards stalking down the corridor every five minutes, seven locks to just open the door. Cold drafts of air sliced around like disoriented snakes, sometimes breezing past our faces and hands, sometimes just coiling around the bars.

For a while we didn't say anything, although words hung heavy in the air.

How are we supposed to stop an army? Should we have chosen life servitude rather than this?

"I couldn't actually tell that George's drink was poisoned," Tanner confessed quietly, "I heard a servant talking about it on the way up."

I waited. Tanner very rarely admitted things he didn't know, all part of his lifelong dedication to becoming a legend. If he was sharing this, it's because he felt like he had something important to say.

"So, of course, I didn't know which mug was poisoned. I made a bad guess apparently."

I sensed a different attitude, so I ventured a comment, "why did you have to drink one at all?"

"To prove my point," Tanner shifted on the ground, turning so he was entirely facing me.

"I will not spend the rest of my life as a stable-hand on a short leash. If the King doesn't approve of me joining you on this mission, you have to convince them."

I avoided his gaze, "What would I say? You keep me alive? If it weren't for you I probably wouldn't be in any risky situations. Ever."

I wasn't saying I wouldn't try to convince them, but Tanner took it that way.

"Are you kidding? I'm the only reason you've had enough money to buy food. You can die of starvation as easily as anyone else. Besides, you'd need me, you know you would."

I cast him a disbelieving look.

"I am the best espionage artist in the kingdom–"

"That's why you die so much."

"–and no one else could get you through an entire army to reach the piper. Besides, I have experience dying! I could throw myself in front of arrows and swords and all that to keep you alive! Everyone else would flinch away."

Tanner's voice had risen with urgency, and the emotion in his turn led me to shift so I could face him.

"You don't actually think the army would attack us. We're just kids."

"They aren't in their right minds. If the piper told them to attack us, they would. Without question. I'm not afraid of it anymore, I'm not afraid of dying"

His tone was almost perfectly casual, but the way he said 'anymore' betrayed him. He tried so hard to seem fearless.

"So what you're saying is you have experience dying, so you can keep me alive?" I was partially jesting, calling out the absurdity in his logic.

"Exactly. You need me."

Tanner didn't blink as he said those words. Just looked at me, trying to convince me that what he was saying was true.

I shifted to sit back against the wall.

"I'll make sure they let you come."

"Don't forget to tell them I'm an espionage expert."

"Have no fear, I won't forget."

We stopped talking, but the dungeon was by no means quiet. The murderer in the next cell over moaned quietly, snores echoed from down the hallway, and there was a steady mechanical banging.

The guards came by later to put out the lamps, although they left the intermittent torches lit.

"Sleep well, we have to be able to save the world tomorrow."

I nodded as I stepped over to the cot, "I'll keep that in mind."

"Oh, and Edy, if you want a different nickname you'll have to come up with a better one."

I didn't sleep well that night, the barrage of new sounds and smells kept me awake and alert. Not to mention the terrifying supposition that nothing was as it should be.

It didn't hit me until the four-o'clock mental breakdown that this job was slightly crazy. I'd heard of other criminals sent to do jobs, but normally it was clearing forests for roads. The lesser criminals were sometimes drafted into the army, but even that was different.

I was going to the eastern reaches of the kingdom to stop a siren. No big deal. I'm sure they'd provide maps, and training of some kind, and all that. They'd have to, like they said, we were stupid teenagers.

"Can you panic a little quieter? I can hear your gears turning from here," Tanner mumbled.

"What if we fail though? What if the piper arrives here and controls everyone? What if even after we defeat the piper they all live as zombies the rest of their lives? What if he discovers how to control kids too? What if he has them all choke themselves? What if the world ends tomorrow?" I wasn't genuinely scared of those things. Not all of them, at least.

"Shut up and go to sleep."

I sighed, heavily enough I knew Tanner would hear it.

The next day we were woken early.

Tanner was escorted outside, where we presumed they'd be testing his ability. I was taken to the library.

It wasn't much larger than Joey's, but apparently the castle had several.

A series of studious men and women in oddly styled clothing 'briefed' me on the basics of the mission.

I simplified it in my head so I wouldn't forget. The mission was as follows: travel along the Alte Straße, meeting with agents of Kingsman at every town along the way to get updates and further instruction on where to go, find the Pied Piper's army, stop the Pied Piper. Sadly I didn't even simplify the last one, my instructors had no more idea than I did.

They also taught me how to take apart a flute. It was riveting.

A guard, with a face like a moldy gourd, had me run and walk laps around a palace garden. It wasn't all that difficult, but I did manage to trip into an elegant plater and scatter the delicate pink flowers everywhere (the gardener snipped at the topiaries particularly fiercely after that).

I caught occasional glimpses of a tall person who might've been Joey, and a short figure that was probably Ginger. They were doing their own run-walk on a stretch of the greenest grass I'd ever seen. I imagined walking the innumerable stairs of the palace would've been a better workout.

The gourd—guard—escorted me back into the palace, where Marie began to bustle me to the smaller library. We ducked into a secret passage, and after she checked the coast was clear she started talking quickly and quietly.

"I believe all of your friends have been approved to accompany you. George, Kingsman I mean, tried to collect a group of young soldiers to accompany you. Apparently they are all too old and the King said you will be escorted only by your friends." Marie said King like it was a dirty word.

"We told him it was impractical, but he insisted," she lowered her voice even further, "rest assured Kingsman has arranged for a company of soldiers to meet you when you arrive in the East."

I nodded, afraid to say anything, for fear I would talk too loud.

She started walking again, and we stepped out from behind a bookshelf into the library. It was stuffy, and motes of dust drifted through the air. There was an unpleasant smell, less like books and more like body odor, that permeated the room.

Around a shelf I could see one of the oddly clothed men standing at a table. He was leaning forward and talking animatedly with someone else. As we came around the table I recognized Joey.

After a day of running laps he looked a little worse for wear. His usually impeccable clothing was wrinkled and there was a sizable grass stain on his left side. His hair was frizzing out of his man bun, strands hanging in front of his eyes.

"Joey! How're you doing!"

"I'm doing well," he glanced up from his book, "you have straw in your hair."

I combed through my hair with my fingers, "That'll be from my cell."

Joey smiled his eyes already scanning the book again, "I can't believe I'm friends with an honest to goodness criminal."

"Two, actually. Tanner's here somewhere."

The professorial man passed a thick tome across the table to Joey.

Joey picked it up, "We're looking for any precedent to the Pied Piper. The reports concluded that he used his music to take control of the adults. Only the adults."

I stepped up to the table, and Marie retreated through the secret passage.

"So, what have you figured out so far?"

The man cleared his throat, "It's a limited enchantment, clearly, by its nature it's more likely to have been cast by a witch than an enchantress."

I disliked the man almost immediately, his voice was nasally and abrasive, not to mention he spoke like I knew what he was talking about.

"You'll have to dumb it down for me a little bit. Is their

instrument enchanted, or is it the piper themself?" When the man showed every intention of explaining I spoke the rest of my clarifying questions louder, "what exactly classifies a limited enchantment? Why should we care if it's a witch or an enchantress?"

The man made a face like sucking on a lemon. I suppose he found my ignorance bitter. I didn't care for it much either.

Joey didn't let him explain. He was tactful enough to understand I'd likely end up shouting at the nerd if he tried to explain.

"Witches can enchant people, not just objects, that means that the piper likely has the power ingrained in him, which makes it harder to stop him. We know his ability is limited because he's only possessed adults, and because witches tend to have less complex enchantments. This is important because it means that the piper can't learn to have any more power than whatever he currently has."

To stop the piper we'd have to somehow incapacitate him. That wasn't my favorite idea, it would've been much easier to steal his pipe, I was a professional in that field.

"That seems like quite a lot to know, what else are you looking for?"

"The population of Kartoffelstadt would be helpful, if he's amassing an army we need to know how many people he has."

"Does it matter? We're only targeting him, right?"

Joey shrugged, "The King thought it would be helpful."

I tapped my fingers on the table. I felt somewhat out of

place. What exactly was I doing in the library? I couldn't help research, and if they were trying to bring me into the know, shouldn't Ginger and Tanner have been there?

"Is there anything I can help with?"

The sour-faced-man passed me a book absently.

I gritted my teeth. Joey pulled the book over into his stack.

"I was thinking you'd like to see this."

He passed me another book and I would've threatened to beat him up, until I saw the page it was open to.

A detailed diagram was inked in pen. I leaned over the page, trying to understand the arrows.

"There are some traps along the Alte Straße, left over from the Red Rebellion five years ago. I'm helpless when it comes to mechanics, as is Hans here, so if you could figure out how they work it would be helpful."

I knew he understood the diagram better than he let on, but I appreciated his kindness.

"Are you planning to disable them, or set them up so we can use them against the army?"

"When the rebellion was stopped we got all the rebels' plans here, so we have maps of where all the traps are. They haven't been a serious problem, so removing them has never been a priority. If we understand what they do we can decide how best to deal with them."

"The Red Rebellion was led by Daemon John who is famous for his traps. It's mainly because of him that we sustained so many casualties during the fight."

I think Hans kept talking but I tuned him out, focusing on the diagram.

It was ingenious really. I suppose the King's protectors must've thought something similar, because they'd copied some of his designs on the wall machines I'd seen.

There were nearly twenty diagrams of different designs and traps.

Joey had me explain how they worked, what they did, and how to disable them. He noted the basics onto a piece of paper. The words were elegant, whether or not I knew what they meant.

When we finished, I was brought back to my straw mattress. The murderer had been cleared out of the cell next to me. A guard with onion on his breath said he'd been hanged that day.

It was standard for traitors and the worst kinds of criminals. Still, it left a sour taste on my tongue.

"I think Joey and Ginger are planning to join us," I told Tanner.

"Idiots. Remind me, who is Ginger?"

"My best friend?"

Tanner put a hand over his heart, "I'm hurt. Do you think so little of me?"

"I mean, you're a tie for second best."

"A tie! With who?"

"Joey, of course."

"Of course," Tanner snorted, "also, bestie isn't a good description for Ginger. I still have no idea who she is."

"She's the one who nearly broke your wrist when you tried

to pick-pocket her."

"The blonde one? Seems a little disingenuous to call a blonde Ginger."

"Whatever. She's coming with us to stop this piper guy, speaking of which," I explained everything Joey had said. Not actually everything, and probably with a lot smaller words, but Tanner got the gist of it.

"I'm getting more excited the more I hear. This is going to be one epic trip."

"You make it sound like a vacation and not a sentencing."

"It's an opportunity Edy, try to be a little positive."

"I think I came up with a better nickname, PS."

"Ken? Mancy?" Tanner injected his voice with enthusiasm.

I laughed, "Mancy?"

"Yeah, like necromancy."

"That's horrible. I was thinking Kay would work."

"That's like you calling me T. It's just weird."

"Not just the letter, K-A-Y."

"Nope, too weird."

"What about Rissa?"

"Where does that come from?"

"My middle name."

"Don't tell me it's Nerissa."

"Shut up, it's not that bad of a name!" I flicked him through the bars.

He shied away, "Sea nymph? Your middle name means sea nymph?"

"It's pretty!"

"And so cheesy."

"It doesn't matter. You can call me Rissa or Kay, or just call me by name."

"Rissa just doesn't sound like you."

"Kay it is then."

"I don't know…"

Someone down the corridor growled, "shut up or I'll strangle you both."

Tanner laid down on his straw cot, "Party pooper."

Chapter 5
The Piper

I first met Daemon near the starch mill. The momentum of my procession carried me there. By then I'd realized I didn't need to keep repeating the tune. Once they were under my control, they remained that way.

The crowd parted to allow Daemon through. He had a face like a snake, with a square and protruding nose, and a forehead and chin that sunk into his neck. He had sharp shrewd eyes the color of ice. He was wearing a clumsily dyed purple tunic. Purple, the color of wealth and Kings.

I gripped my penny whistle fast, just in case he made any sharp moves.

"This is an impressive army you've gathered." He had a voice the color of power.

"What do you want?" with a thought, I commanded the adults to step in closer, in case they needed to protect me.

"Hello to you too, I'm Daemon," His accent was faintly

northern, "As for what I want...depends on what you want."

Daemon had been clustered around the mill with several dirty men, also in hand-dyed tunics. They pushed their way into the crowd to flock around him. They were built less like blacksmiths and more like long distance runners, with muscles that were taut against the bone, leaving knobbly knees and elbows.

"I want to be King."

The valley was quieter than it had any right to be, only Daemon's men were shuffling, only Daemon's men dared breathe. The villagers were standing so close to me I felt their heat, but they were statues. Their clothing was buffeted about by the small wind, with a sound like rattling leaves.

Daemon licked his lips, increasing his likeness to a reptile, "You already have an impressive group here. You may not need it but I want to help. Do you remember the Red Rebellion?"

I remembered it well. We'd lived off weeds most of that year.

"We lost fifty men over the course of an eight month war, the King lost hundreds. Let me be your general."

I want you to know I wasn't entirely a fool. I knew he wouldn't be content as a general. He wanted to be King, he wanted power.

Regardless, I knew I had no expertise. An experienced rebel leader would be nice to have. My men had lost their individuality, their skills. They couldn't pay the tab at a hotel, or come up with plans, or even know which direction to go.

The snake had voluntarily slid its way into my hands, I just had to clutch it tightly enough it couldn't bite me. Still, I didn't like the image of the slick thing winding in and out between my fingers, up my arm, eventually tightening around my throat. I could practically feel the scales rubbing against my skin, but I held out my hand.

"Plug your ears," I said as I shook his hand.

His beady eyes bulged. He clamped his hands over his ears.

I raised my flute and played three sharp notes. The men who'd been following Daemon all stilled, standing as stiff and unnatural as the villagers at my back.

When I lowered the flute Daemon lowered his hands, his expression wary, "My men were loyal to me, they wouldn't have attacked you."

Hiss hiss little snake.

"Loyal to you. I want an army that obeys me."

Daemon's head was angled downward, so when he met my eyes he was staring through his lashes, a disquieting expression playing across his face.

"As you will, my liege," the serpent bowed.

So, you see, that's all it took. To gain the respect of adults, to gain followers. A little magic, a little anger, and a goal.

Daemon explained the fastest route to the capital was along the Alte Straße, and if we kept a fast pace it could take as few as three weeks, but safe, and slightly slower travel, would take up to five.

Alte Straße didn't lead directly to Kartoffelstadt, so we'd have to travel along minor roads until we intersected the path.

Oak trees provided us shelter, a thick carpet of leaves under our feet, and branches arching over our heads. They were in the golden splendor of autumn, vibrant yellows, oranges, and reds formed a new sky.

I played a few notes as we walked, comforted by the way the sound wove around the thick trunks and played through the limbs.

Daemon covered his ears, though I had no intention of enslaving him. I made sure to keep several people between us, just in case he tried something funny.

Slowly my grip on that snake would loosen, he'd begin to spiral closer and closer to my neck, but not yet. He was still maintaining his distance, until he could spring one of the traps he was so famous for.

Chapter 6
Kennedy

My hands were pinned before I was even fully awake. My eyes flew open, and in the dim light of a torch I could see a figure kneeling over me. Their legs had my hands pinned on either side of my body and silver knives glinted in their hands. Light reflected off my assailant's eyes as they glowered down at me.

I kicked ineffectually, and tried to wrench my hands free. No joy.

My next instinct was to scream, but the enemy must've seen that intention in my eyes, because as quick as blinking they tucked a knife into their belt, and covered my mouth with a gloved hand.

I bucked as they lowered the other knife toward my neck. I managed to free a hand. They lost their balance, and I clapped them on the ear.

They yelped, and slashed with the knife.

My cheek seared with pain and I cried out.

I threw them off me, scooting back against the wall, and

using it as a crutch to help me rise. My feet were knocked out from underneath me, and my head cracked against the wall as I collapsed.

I kicked blindly, and the attacker grunted in pain.

"Edy? Edy!?" I could barely hear Tanner's voice over the pounding in my ears.

"Help!" I called, scrambling to my feet again. This time I managed to dodge as the attacker attempted to sweep my feet out from under me.

A knife was sent clattering across the stone, and I dove for it.

I grabbed it and awkwardly rolled to my feet, raising it in a defensive position. I wasn't particularly stable, or skilled with a knife, and it was lucky my terrified expression was hidden in shadow.

Something shiny flew at my face. I tried to block it with my knife instead of dodging, and the thing lodged in my arm.

I screamed, a gargled mix of pain and anger.

I passed the knife I was holding to my other hand. Then I ran at the attacker, hoping my adrenaline would make up for lack of talent. I tackled them to the floor, but didn't manage to pin them down.

Before I knew what was happening, my good hand was pinned under their boot, the knife ripped from my grip. I tried to move my other hand to shove away their boot, and a sharp pain tore up my arm.

They toppled off me anyway, and after a moment of panic, I realized Tanner had reached through the bars and was holding onto

62

the assassin by their hair. Tanner adjusted his grip, until his fingers were clamped around the person's neck.

I had a moment to catch my breath, and in the sudden stillness, I caught a glimpse of the attacker's face. Their motive immediately became clear.

The man had a cloth wrapped around the lower half of their face, and purple gemstones were stitched into their skin along their hairline. They had the inner glow of enchanted things.

"You ok Edy?"

"Kay."

"Good, do you think—"

"No, I meant call me Kay. I am not ok, I got hit by a knife."

"Could you just call for a guard," Tanner spoke through gritted teeth. The assailant was struggling against Tanner's grip.

"They'll be coming already," I said.

I stepped forward, and kicked the man in the head, just as he broke free of Tanner's grasp.

While he was reeling I caught his flailing arms and shoved them through the bars to Tanner, who twisted them behind the man's head. The assailant was still gasping for air as I knelt beside him.

I yanked the knife out of my arm, hissing as I did, and held the point to the man's forehead. He wasn't afraid of death, so I threatened him with something worse.

"Tell me something," I growled, applying pressure, "would you risk your eternal life for this mission?" I pried, and the gemstone twisted.

The man was obviously a member of Befreiung der
Verdammten. The most dangerous religious cult of the era. They
had members across the known world, all united under the dogma
that eternal life could be achieved through the use of twisted
magicks. They enchanted gemstones with qualities, and embedded
them into their bodies. When they died, they believed their spirits
rose from the grave and could inhabit the bodies of the weak
willed or lacking in power. They wore the gemstones to grant them
that power, and also to guarantee that they couldn't be taken by
other members.

Naturally, the cult had originated in the Northern mountains.
The beliefs had grown from the gruesome stories of children
sprouting second heads, and people who slowly sank in on
themselves, until they metamorphosed into someone else.

Based on the fact that the cultists considered themselves
immortal, they were unphased by death, and unafraid to go on
suicide missions for their leaders. The leader was said to have risen
seventeen times, and apparently offered irrefutable proof they had
the same soul.

"You wouldn't," the man breathed.

I twisted and a single gemstone clattered across the ground.
The man cried out, and blood beaded up.

He writhed, "No!"

"Why were you sent here?"

"I won't tell you."

I dug into the next gemstone.

"Yes you will, or I'll cut each of these out of your face and

64

kill you for good."

The man whimpered, but the sound evoked no pity.

"What you do is unnatural. The Leaders want to end you."

Members of Befreiung der Verdammten never said they killed people, because it didn't denote the completion of the progression. Instead they said end, as if it were a fairy tale.

"How did you get into the palace?" The paranoid king would no more allow his kind in than a rabid bear.

"I hid myself in a wagon of food. They delivered me to the kitchen," the man had a rough voice, and it only got rougher after he coughed.

"Edy, can you please make sure the guards are coming? This guy is as wriggly as an eel," Tanner asked through the bars.

"Just a second," I had an idea, and I think Tanner knew, because he didn't protest.

I popped a second gemstone out of his head, ignoring his protest. I wiped the blood on the corner of my shirt, and collected the other from the floor.

I rolled them through my fingers a few times, before popping them into my mouth.

"I may be unnatural," the gemstones clinked against my teeth as I spoke, "but trust me," I swallowed, "I'm your only shot at living forever."

The man was staring agape at me, so I pressed my forearm into his neck. I held it there until he relaxed, and still didn't let go, until he stopped pretending and actually passed out.

It wasn't nice, but I hadn't gotten into the criminal

underground by being kind. We needed to be strong to survive, and sometimes being ruthless was the best way to show strength– twisted or not.

I wrapped the face mask around the boy's forehead, where blood was still welling up where I'd removed the gemstones. I say boy, because with the lower half of his face revealed he was clearly much younger than I'd previously thought.

The guards arrived then, and two took the knives the boy had brought. They left the last one, a scrawny guard who could barely walk in his armor, to throw the boy over his shoulder and stumble after them down the hall. Before he could, however, he had to lock the cell, which was an excruciating affair of him fumbling for and dropping his keys several times.

When they'd disappeared down the hall, I spat the jewels out of my mouth.

"He could've killed me right?" I went to wipe my bloody cheek, and only succeeded in aggravating both it, and the stab wound in my arm.

Tanner hesitated, "Yes, I'd say he could've."

"I guess you proved your worth. No one can doubt that you should come now."

"My worth should've been obvious," Tanner's voice became softer, "You should probably wrap your arm before you bleed out."

I shrugged and sat against the wall.

"Why did you take the second jewel?" Tanner asked quietly. He was only quiet when he thought I'd done something wrong, so I was immediately defensive.

"I didn't take any of the ones they consider essential, only the expensive ones."

They were smaller than my pinky fingernail, but they had a certain weight to them. I held my hand through the bars, and Tanner took them from my palm.

"Which one was the first?" Tanner was holding them up to see the light reflecting through them.

"Loved," I'd felt it. That was the thing about enchantments, most were hard to understand unless you felt the emotional power of the things. Some people claimed the words were written in the way light scattered across the surface, but as I was illiterate, it wouldn't have helped me.

"I bet that one cost a pretty penny. If I was reborn loved by everyone, it would be pretty great."

"We could probably pawn it for a good amount. The second would probably be worth more though."

"What is it?" Tanner had put down the first one to feel the second better. He pinched it between his thumb and index finger.

"Squint a little harder and you'll feel it," I teased.

Tanner shot me a glare, "All I feel is annoyed."

"Luck. It's luck."

Tanner closed his eyes for a second, trying to focus.

"I don't feel it."

A defensive tone had crept back into my voice, "You always struggle to sense it. Remember the cursed coin?"

"That doesn't count. Curses are different."

"They are so not," I reached through the bars and grabbed

the gemstones back.

"I can't believe you put them in your mouth," Tanner made a disgusted face.

"I had to make a point."

Tanner mimed gagging.

"I did! He may have a future if we get him away from that sick cult."

"Befreiung der Verdammten? I don't know if it's possible, they're pretty devoted," Tanner looked over to meet my eyes and sighed, "Seriously Kennedy, you need to do something to stop the bleeding."

"Head wounds always bleed a lot. He barely nicked me."

"What about your arm?"

I looked down at it, "I'll admit it hurts a bit."

"And it's bleeding bucketfuls."

"Not bucketfuls, surely."

A voice from the darkness down the hall spoke up, "Blood?"

Tanner and I silently agreed to stop talking.

I tore a strip of fabric from the shoddy blanket in the cell.

I wrapped my arm tightly, but I didn't really bother to make it look neat. I assumed Marie would probably have it bandaged tomorrow.

Sleep came quickly. I suppose it was a byproduct of blood loss.

The nightmares came fast too. I was standing on the palace grounds, with a mechanical beast chasing me, forcing me to run laps. Then I tripped into a fountain of gemstones and started to drown. The worst part wasn't the lack of breath, it was the tough sharpness of the crystals as they scraped down my throat and dropped into my stomach.

The next few days were a blur. Marie really did bandage my arm, but not until she'd sterilized the wound with bitter alcohol. Joey spent most of the time in the library, but the General had made it clear Joey had passed the physical, and would be joining us. Ginger too was going, but I didn't get to see her. In all her prudence, she'd decided to spend as long as she could at home brewing potions for the trip. That's not what she told Kingsman of course, she said her mother was sick and she had to make sure she recovered before we left.

Tanner spent the time beside me, learning to throw a knife, use a sword, and in a pinch, the basics of wrestling. He was better at all of them than I was, which was frustrating to no end. I was faster than him in the distance running, but I hated it more than he did too, so I'm not sure if that was a good thing or not.

The King was occasionally visible peering out of some terrace or another to observe us. Tanner would wave at him, and he'd immediately disappear out of sight.

It was nearly middle night when they kicked us out for good.

Joey and Tanner were strapped into giant backpacks that held food, tents, and medical kits. I was given a smaller bag, where I carried my own water bottle, iodine tablets, and a few random knick-knacks. Ginger had a similar bag, but she'd loaded it with thermoses and bottles of potions.

We were instructed to follow the road until we reached

Kneipenstadt.

I'd asked about horses, but apparently the road was thin through the mountains and horses couldn't be trusted. Just as ominous, we apparently had to cross a lot of misty rope bridges that hadn't been serviced in years.

Every hero story I'd ever been told had some kind of wicked rope bridge. Not to say I was scared. I was just wary of falling through a rotted board and to my death.

We had a three hour walk until we could even get to the real road we'd follow.

I guess hero stories were on my mind that day, because I started to get annoyed as I stumbled for the thirtieth time. The heroes were always traveling the world, in a series of short words. Sometimes as short as, 'they traveled long and hard' or 'they crossed the mountains'.

I can see why. Walking for hours on end is nearly the least climactic thing that could ever happen. I could recount every peril of the walk–am I going to trip over this stone? Is this a snake or a stick–but that would be nearly as boring.

"If I was a poet this would be much more interesting," Joey said. It was the first thing anyone had said since "it's way too early for this" so we all eagerly jumped on the dialogue.

"How so?" I asked.

"Reminiscing about all your noble lovers?" Ginger sighed.

"Weirdo," Tanner laughed.

"Well, if I were a poet I could make clever remarks about the way the wind is a warning, or how the trees all bend toward us like they're enthralled in our story," he turned to give Ginger a pointed look, "I wouldn't be a love poet. They're much too absorbed in the physical, too little in the metaphoric."

Ginger snorted, "please. Love may be a physical thing in those stuffy books you read, but in real life, it's more metaphoric than 'the wind as a warning'."

"If you use like or as it's a simile," Joey muttered.

"So?" Ginger was in a debating mood, and her eyes glinted with excitement

"You said in real life love is more metaphoric than wind as a warning. It's not metaphoric at all, it's a simile."

"But metaphoric doesn't relate only to metaphor, it relates to figurative language. Simile falls under that category."

"By its very name metaphoric relates to metaphor."

"There's no word for simile-ic. It doesn't exist. It falls under metaphoric so there was no need to invent another word."

"That's a logical fallacy. You have no way to prove the reason simile-ic was never invented as a word."

Tanner groaned, "talking about grammar is probably the only thing more boring than just walking."

"Shut up, I like the debate," I replied.

Tanner rolled his eyes, "Then let's debate something better."

"What's your suggestion?" Joey asked, at the same time as Ginger said, "How can you determine that the subject is objectively better?"

"Why not argue—"

"It's not an argument, it's a debate."

"—about how to stop the Pied Piper. That would be useful and interesting, and thus objectively better," Tanner hopped a few steps, trying to shake a rock out of his shoe.

"That's more of planning than argument. If you insist, my position is that we should prepare for spontaneity. If we leave all options open, we'll be able to react to whatever the situation is like when we arrive," Ginger adjusted her backpack.

"Planning would be very effective actually, but I agree that it's not really a debate at this point. Better, is it right to call the enchanter the Pied Piper?" Joey wasn't smiling, but there was a happiness etched into the lines of his expression.

Tanner dramatically mimed dying of boredom.

"How do you mean?" Ginger asked.

"Well, pied means multicolored—"

"Skip the definition part and get to the morality part," Ginger insisted.

"Very well. If the piper has some kind of vitiligo, which is where I assume the nickname pied came from, it's offensive to call them pied. Whether or not they're a good person, they shouldn't be known for the look of their skin."

Ginger sighed, "Why did you have to base your argument on such a good basis? No matter what I say I'll seem immoral and horrible for being against you!"

"Maybe the term pied has nothing to do with his skin," I figured, "maybe his pipe has multiple colors. Or his cloak or something."

Joey made a contemplative sound, "that may be true, they

didn't specify what the instrument looked like. If it's made of wood, there is a good chance it has multiple colors, and thus the term pied could be applied without any impoliteness."

"Who cares about being polite? We're trying to stop a hypnotized army from destroying the kingdom. What we call the piper doesn't matter," Tanner said, with a distinct air of exasperation.

"I disagree," Ginger smirked at Tanner's visible annoyance, "calling him a piper identifies him as what he is, and that is of the utmost importance. If we just call him The Man there's no clarity in his identity. He could be any member of the army."

"Which brings up an interesting point, what if there are other instruments in the army? Don't some soldiers carry drums?" I asked.

"I wonder if his spell could extend to the music they play… "Joey's voice trailed off, and we all knew we'd lost him. He'd be thinking over that for the next several minutes.

Ginger elbowed me, "Come on! You've distracted my debate partner!"

"Thank heavens," Tanner said. Ginger elbowed him too, but with the huge pack he was wearing, he toppled over.

"Not cool," He said, struggling to right himself.

"It's actually very cool," I said, tugging on his pack and helping him to his feet.

"Can you two please just stop debating things? Can't you tell stories, or jokes, or just walk?"

"What are we, jesters? We aren't your entertainment."

Ginger flipped her hair.

"I actually have a really good story to tell. Have I ever told you about the second time Tanner died?"

Tanner yelped, "Really Edy?"

Ginger's eyes glittered as she smiled at me, "Edy huh?"

"Hey! I was going to make fun of Tanner! Don't turn this back on me!"

"Ok ok ok, how did Tanner die the second time," Ginger linked her arm in mine,

"He was trying to steal a blue fruit from one of the exotic vendors," I started, "so he pretended to trip into the cart, except he'd miscalculated and he actually tripped over his feet."

Tanner started singing a drinking song very loudly to hide my voice.

"He knocked the cart over a stone and the fruit went flying everywhere…"

"Pass me another round bartender!"

"..and I mean everywhere. Children were darting into the square and running off with all the fruits. The vendor tried to come around the cart to attack him. Did I mention that this exotic vendor was from the North? He was waving around a thick butcher knife, one already stained with blood…"

"Cause I wanna forget my troubles!"

"So Tanner decided he'd just book it out of the square…"

Tanner's efforts intensified, until he was screeching loudly in our ears, "I lost my heart in a game of dice!"

"…and he stepped on one of the fruits, fell, and conked his

head on the cart."

"It wasn't worth a ton so I'm still in debt!" I was pretty sure he was making up the song as he went.

"The vendor came around and went to threaten Tanner, so he tried to knock the knife out of his hand. He was dizzy after hitting his head so hard, but he still managed to knock the knife out of the man's hand…"

"So pass me another round bartender!"

"…and it fell right onto him. The end."

Ginger laughed, "he didn't even try to get out of the way?"

"No! And even better, everyone in the square but him got a blue fruit."

Tanner stopped singing, "That's not even how it really happened."

"Then how did it happen?" Ginger asked.

Joey snapped out of his trance just then, "just like Kennedy explained actually. And Tanner, you can't just combine two songs like that. You butchered them both."

"You're supposed to be on my side!"

Joey shrugged, "Sorry Tanner."

We kept walking at about the same pace, needling Tanner the whole way. He was just so easy to make fun of, he tried so hard to be cool. We tried Joey for a minute, but he took it and said he accepted the logic of our jokes, so it was no fun.

Ginger was remarkably fun to tease though. She was passionate enough to defend herself well, but also innately funny enough to laugh at. Her many love interests were the best topic of discussion. There was the foreign prince she said was wealthy enough, but way too much drama. There was the palace guard, who she said was a good kisser but also too thick to debate anything. Not to mention the bard, the spy, and the rich one who turned out to be a member of Befreiung der Verdammten, although Ginger never admitted where she'd found the gemstones.

The problem with teasing her was that she knew enough about my personal life that she posed a legitimate threat to my dignity. Everytime she brought up something I knew Tanner could bother me about I stopped annoying her and started defending her.

Despite my efforts, I was, of course, beat up too. Tanner had apparently seen me fall out of the tree, both times, which really entertained Ginger. Joey recounted the time I'd snuck into a dance at his house, and ended up locking myself in the prison. Ginger was bound from telling the best stories to tease her about, because of an oath we'd taken when we turned twelve.

Eventually we did reach Alte Straße, and when we did we could've leapt for joy. It wasn't a big deal that we'd reached it, I suppose, but it was a change of course, and proof that we'd been going in the right direction.

Only ten minutes down it, however, all our elation was gone. It was indeed a very old road. It was uneven and worn, wagon's had left deep ruts in the road. Weeds tickled our ankles, and gave us the sensation of bugs crawling up our legs. Sometimes it wasn't even a phantom sensation; ants hung in bunches at the top of longer grass, just waiting to attack.

Chapter 7
Kennedy

We reached the town late at night, and found the Kingsman's agent. He was a grizzled old man, and his face seemed set in an expression of boredom. I barely even heard what he said, I was too busy watching his face to see if he ever showed emotion. As far as I could tell, only the speed at which he tapped his foot revealed anything.

He'd purchased us two rooms for the night. Joey had prepared for some minor inconveniences, but he'd never had to stay in a cheap inn before, let alone shared a room.

"Don't we need four?" He asked.

The man's expression didn't even flicker, but his tapping became more agitated, "Weren't expecting to be treated like a King were ya?"

Joey blinked, "Oh, I suppose not."

We separated into our respective rooms. Ginger and I got the larger room, despite Tanner's attempts to get it from us.

I offered to take the floor but Ginger insisted that my sleep was much more important. In the end, I got the mattress, but she had the pillow and blanket.

I thought it would be hard to fall asleep, with the whole saving the world thing on my shoulders, but a day of walking is apparently tiring.

The next morning we set off before the tavern served breakfast, so we snacked on jerky as we walked.

We reached the next Inn well into the witching hours. We found our rooms and dropped of our bags before we went to the tavern to meet with the agent.

This one was younger than the rest, probably only a few years older than we were. He had the build of a person who hadn't quite grown into their bones yet.

After brief introductions–his name was Tad–he gave us our instructions for the next day's walk. Essentially, keep following the Alte Straße. We would pass through two small villages, but we couldn't stop because the locals were known for their brutality toward travelers. Tad also warned us that adders were common along the dryer patches of road.

The next morning Tad woke us up by kicking our doors, "Rise and shine, it's trekking time!"

We couldn't complain that it was too early for such needless pep, because it wasn't actually all that early. The birds had already finished their morning songs, and the sun beat down on us as we walked.

Tad hadn't been all that dislikable when we'd met him, but

we found a way to be frustrated with him as we walked. He'd neglected to tell us that the two villages full of angry people celebrated the Summer Festival for three weeks. It wasn't an uncommon practice in rural areas, so we could have assumed, but we had Tad to blame so we were perfectly content to be annoyed at someone else.

Tanner and I had been complaining about Tad good naturedly–Tanner did a wonderful impression of the way Tad bounced on his toes–and Joey tried to stop our trash talk.

"It's only a tad Tad's fault," He said.

It was one of those phrases that's so perfect for the situation that it becomes an immediate inside joke. Not because it was particularly funny, but few inside jokes are ever *really* funny.

We had to leave the Alte Straße to walk the alleyways through the villages, to avoid being trampled by their huge swing dances. Tanner did pop into one shop briefly to nick a few sweet rolls, which we barely got to enjoy, because an angry shopkeep started chasing us and we had to digest the evidence.

The next agent of Kingsman was Tad's twin brother Tog. Tog looked, in most ways, similar to Tad except that Tog was trying to grow a beard. He was also much less energetic than his brother.

Ginger took an immediate liking to him–apparently she liked his 'aura'--and we ended up waiting in the tavern for several hours while she talked to him before we could disappear to our rooms. Tanner, Joey, and I were talking separately, and one of us happened to mention that something was only a tad Tad's fault, and Tog must've heard because we were on our way to our rooms the next second.

We didn't pass through any villages that next day. Tog had warned us about wasp nests that were under stones and in crevices, and we did find several of them. We had to sprint for our lives every once in a while to escape them.

Worse, Tanner stirred up an adder, and only thanks to Ginger's extensive conversation with Tog, did we know what to do.

Making things more difficult, we'd passed through the flats and were trekking through the much less hospitable hills. Ginger's optimism had suggested it would provide welcome variety, but it wasn't as welcome as she'd hoped.

We reached the next town before the sun had really set.

"Finally! We can get a full night's rest!" Tanner dumped his backpack ceremoniously on the bed.

We were all excited, but then it turned out that we couldn't really get a full night's rest. A heat wave was predicted, so we had to get going during the night so we could avoid the worst of it.

As it happens, the prediction had been incorrect. It had absolutely nothing to do with Tad, but it was still a tad his fault the entire time.

The hills had slowly changed from rolling to steep, and we were exhausted from the constant uphill. Wasps nests were still constant traps, and every time one of us stomped on one, we had to take off running up the steep slopes.

After one such sprint, we came to the crest of a hill, panting and dry heaving. It took us a moment before we even noticed the valley ahead of us.

"Is this..." Ginger trailed off in depressed silence.

My mind filled in the rest, where they all went? And by they, I meant all the children abandoned by the possessed adults.

They curled up under raggedy blankets, their faces covered in layers of dirt and dust. Sweat and tears had left tracks on their faces, and I couldn't help but think how it made them look like their faces were melting.

Some kids were chasing bugs around on the hillside, some were playing hopping games. The area echoed with their shouts, and the quiet sobbing of hundreds of others.

A taller boy, probably about our age–although I was always bad at estimating age–was standing closest to us.

Joey cleared his throat, "Are you from Kartoffelstadt?"

The boy looked at Joey appraisingly, "Yeah. Wha d'ya want?"

Joey cleared his throat again, and crossed his hands over his chest, "We're on our way to meet the adults from Kartoffelstadt. The King has asked us to–"

"You sound rich, ya rich?" other kids were starting to gather behind the boy, "You have food in those sacs? We could use sommit to eat."

Joey seemed at a loss for words. He was used to people in the capital, who always treated him with the utmost respect, if not for his title, then for the dignified way he spoke.

"We don't have enough food for you all. We can help you get into town though, I'm sure they could feed you," I say, looking to my friends for confirmation. We could walk them back to town, set them up with the Kingsman's agent, and then head out again on our trip.

Maybe a hundred kids were up now, gathering behind the boy like a diminutive army. Their faces were all set in the same expression of determination. They were pressed tight to each other, and the younger ones clung to their siblings or friends with white knuckles.

"How far izzit?" He asked.

A girl shuffled her way through the crowd and shoved the boy aside. By her height alone I assumed she was about our age as well. Even coated in dirt, her hair was lighter in color than anyone else's and when she moved something in it flashed, as though it was dusted with glitter.

"I'm the mayor's daughter, from Kartoffelstadt. What was you saying about the King?" She had the same accent as the boy, but she spoke as if she thought she was much above him.

"You were only the mayor's kid for a day," the boy said, knocking the girl in the side.

"At least someone wanted me."

Ginger, sensing a fight, stepped forward.

"How many of you are hungry!" She spoke loudly, clearly addressing the younger kids, and not just the teens at the front.

There was a moment, filled with the sound of a hundred little feet shuffling. A small girl at the front raised her hand, and soon every kid was holding a hand over their head. Grudgingly the teens followed suit.

"We aven't eaten much since we's left," the boy admitted.

"That's what I thought. Let's make the food a priority, yes?"

She kept talking but my attention had drifted.

There was a boy at the bottom of the hill. He was bent over a bundle of blankets. As I focused on him, I heard strains of the lullaby he was singing.

"I'll be right back," I whispered to Tanner, before jogging down the hill toward the boy.

I slowed before I reached him, trying to keep from startling him.

He kept singing, his voice dry and cracking, even when I came around and knelt beside him. He only stopped when I spoke up.

"Are you ok?"

He lifted his head, and gestured to bring my attention to the bundle he held. He was rocking a small baby back and forth. The boy had managed to keep most of the dirt off of its face, but the baby was clearly sick.

"I know what'll help her," I looked up at my friends, and just caught Ginger giving orders for everyone to gather their stuff to start walking.

I waved to get Ginger's attention, and after the crowd dispersed she hastened down the hill.

"What is it?"

"Do you have any healing medicine?" I would've said potion, but potions were as often associated with dark things as necromancy, and I didn't want to scare the boy.

"Of course," she knelt down and started talking in a lowered voice to the child.

Tanner and Joey joined us a second later.

"We're going to walk them back to the Inn, get them settled," Tanner explained.

I stood up and brushed a few eager ants off my trousers, "sounds great."

Getting that many kids to just walk took more effort than any of us had expected. The younger ones occasionally just sat down in the middle of the road, and refused to continue walking. We carried them on our shoulders, or convinced them to keep walking, but they slowed the pace. What's more, someone started a game of tag that left a gaggle of children scattering every direction. A few kids passed out as we continued, and when they did one of us stayed back to give them water and little bits of our jerky until they were ready to move, and even then we half carried them along the trail. At least the wasps didn't cause too many problems.

When we finally reached the town, we almost looked like wild animals. We were covered by blankets like pelts, choking on dirt, and moving in one giant stumbling mass.

Kingsman's agent was scarily efficient, dividing the children by their needs: the sick ones, the injured ones, and the healthy-ish. Physicians were summoned, and they tended to the former two, the latter was sent to collect from numerous wells, and gather food from several safe houses.

Ginger talked to the youngest kids and kept them entertained, and when the adults' backs were turned she gave them

84

sips of mysterious potions from her bag. Tanner had disappeared, and I hoped–without much faith–that he wasn't off stealing something.

Joey was talking to the teenagers who'd spoken up earlier. He noted what they said in a little journal from his pocket. He was scribbling so excitedly, he snapped his pencil in half, but barely paused to brush the second half from the paper before he continued writing.

By the time all was said and done, it was mid evening. Kingsman's agent, after several hours of useless bustling, gathered us together. She explained that we wouldn't see another soul for the next few days of travel, so we had no reason to dawdle. She did buy us some hard candies to suck on as we walked.

They melted in our palms as we walked and left streaks of bright colors. They reminded me of spring time at home, when my sisters and I visit the wild meadows outside the capital walls and picked the most vibrant flowers we could find to decorate our house. By the end of the spring, the roof was covered in bushes of picked flowers, and the windowsills overflowed with colorful blossoms. They not only served to brighten the street, but also to remind Dad what spring looked like outside the house–he never went outside, so we had to bring outside to him.

The steep hills were no easier the second time, but at least we knew which buzzing holes to avoid. Tanner led the way, with a jauntiness in his walk that wasn't typical.

"What's got you so excited?" I asked.

Tanner grinned and practically skipped along the path, "I'm

just excited to keep moving."

"Sure." I feigned disinterest, as I would if I wanted to get information from any toddler.

Tanner fell for it, "We're traveling at night for the first time."

When I didn't respond Tanner sighed dramatically.

"There are all kinds of animals that hunt at night."

I socked him in the arm, "You're excited because a giant cat might eat you?"

"Please! I have a strength ring, they couldn't hurt me."

"That ring doesn't even work. You had it when the Northerner attacked you, didn't you?"

"Magick doesn't always work on Northerners," he pulled the ring off his finger and held it out to me, "since you're so good at reading enchantments, you can confirm that it's strength."

I didn't close my eyes, but I focused on the ring as we made out way up a hill.

"Fine. It's a strength ring. Maybe it doesn't imbue the user though. Maybe the ring just won't ever fall apart."

"Whatever Rissa. It's better than a luck charm pried from a man's head."

"Oh shut up."

Joey looked at us sharply, "A luck charm?"

Tanner grinned and skipped on ahead.

"Yeah. I took it from a cultist who tried to kill me in prison."

"Befreiung der Verdammten?"

"Yeah, apparently what I do is unholy, and I'm on the 'to be killed' list or something."

Joey was talking rapidly, although he didn't seem to be speaking directly to anyone, "Luck, along with pride, power, and greatness are only for the upper powers—"

Ginger put her arm around my shoulders conspiratorially, "I always knew you'd be the first to get famous."

Tanner scoffed loudly, drowning out Joey's further questions. A heated debate followed, where Tanner essentially listed his many merits and Ginger, with playful vitriol, discredited them all. Joey, always the peace maker, made sure Tanner's feelings didn't get too badly hurt by reminding him we were telling his stories at every Inn we passed.

I jumped in whenever I felt like I had something particularly clever to say, but most of the time I focused on making sure I didn't run into a wasps nest.

We stopped to make camp when Joey tripped over his own feet and stumbled into Ginger, knocking them both to the ground.

There was a decently flat spot, so we attempted to set up the tents. Joey kept explaining how they should work, except we couldn't tie the knots right, and the ropes kept slipping down the tree trunks. There were also thin wooden poles to give added support around the edges, and we couldn't fit them in quite right. Tanner thought it would assemble through sheer application of will, and I was drowning in the fabric as I tried to unfold it and see how it worked.

Ginger laughed heartily at us all as she warmed the dinner over the fire.

Well, she laughed until she realized why there are usually

stone rings around fire pits.

"Ah! Fire!"

Joey whipped around and hopped back like he was scared it would bite him.

"Genius deduction!" Tanner yelped.

I tried to stamp out the fire, but the dry weeds were quickly catching and my foot couldn't keep up.

Tanner shoved me back toward the packs, and stole the tent from my fumbling fingers. He dove onto the fire and tried to smother it.

Unfortunately the tent acted more like a billows, and soon the fire was spreading.

Joey shouted at Tanner from a safe distance, correcting his form.

Ginger poured the contents of our water bottles in a half circle to keep the fire from advancing.

Several panicked minutes later the fireside was a slope of glowing embers. Tanner had minor burns on his fingers and arms, and his hair, which he was so proud of, was slightly singed. Ginger's pride was hurt, but she wasn't physically injured. Joey was only concerned that he would miss a meal.

I was proud we, together, had managed to stop a wildfire, and tried to ignore the fact that we had started it. I was also disgruntled about how Tanner had shoved me away. Sure the effects of my attempt were meager, but it was better than nothing.

When I asked him about it he shrugged, "My job is to keep you alive, or don't you remember? If you burned to death we'd all be doomed."

That made enough sense that I didn't argue.

The tent was entirely useless, so we splayed out on the dirt, sharing the three blankets we had (Joey had apparently traded his out to make room for seven different notebooks, just in case). We used our packs as pillows.

The next day we met our first scary rope bridge.

It was worse than I thought. I'd pictured rotting boards and fraying rope, but I'd pictured four ropes, two to hold the boards, and two as handrails.

Instead there were three. And no boards.

"I am not crossing that with this backpack on," Tanner's declaration was uncharacteristically smart.

"They are much too large, and we'll be off balance…Is there any other way across?

There was, but it would involve two long climbs up and down sheer faces of rock, so none of us brought it up.

"Maybe one of us ferries across the most important goods, in a smaller and more well balanced backpack," Ginger suggested.

Joey coughed, "All my goods are essential."

"If you tighten the straps enough the backpacks shouldn't make you much more unstable, just don't lean back," I said.

Tanner bit his lip but agreed quickly, Joey went about explaining just how impractical it was, Ginger amended my idea until everyone was in agreeance.

We found metal clips in our supplies, and when our turns came, we'd clip ourselves to one of the handrails, and shimmy across as best we could.

Tanner went first, always the gentleman, and he adopted a fully sideways approach. He leaned as far back as he could with the hand-rope, and kept his feet on the main one. He relied almost entirely on the clip to hold his weight as he shuffled to the other side of the gorge.

Joey went next, and he tried walking straight forward. He kept his hands on both handrails, and had his clip attached to the back of his bag so it wouldn't hinder his movement as much. He wobbled a bit, but made it over fine.

Both Joey and Tanner had an advantage over Ginger and I, and not just because of their natural levels of athleticism. They had spent years perfecting their footwork, either as a pickpocket and fugitive, or as a dancer and fencer.

I rarely got close up in thievery, and Ginger spent most of her time standing over a cauldron or sitting at her desk.

Luckily we had something neither Joey or Tanner did. A little bit of magic.

Ginger pulled a small yellow bottle from her bag, "This is my personal specialty. I gathered all the ingredients myself and created my own recipe. It wasn't big enough for all of us to share, but there's enough for both of us."

"What does it do?" I held the vial in front of my eyes and shook it. The colorful fluid inside had a very low viscosity.

She winked, "You'll see."

I swallowed about half the vial, then passed the bottle back to her.

The potion didn't kick in until I was a few steps onto the bridge. I was hit by a shock, like I'd suddenly been dunked under water, and the air changed texture immediately.

I hadn't even realized that air had a texture, until I was standing in something else.

I went to take a step forward, and it felt like I was moving through syrup.

Curious, I made a funky gesture with my hands, and sure enough, it propelled me slightly upwards and off the rope.

I didn't need it to support me anymore, I could swim through the air.

The best part wasn't the sensation of floating, it was the expressions of both Tanner and Joey when I made it to the end.

I think they were talking, but I couldn't hear them because the watery air had filled my ears.

I unclipped myself from the line, and experimentally started to swim upwards over solid ground.

Sure enough, I was practically flying. I mimed walking up invisible steps, and doing the kinds of flips I wished I could do through real air.

Ginger didn't even bother to clip herself in as she swam across. She made it look easy.

I was several feet in the air when my potion wore off, and I stayed there for maybe a full second before I started falling.

"Crap."

The ground rushed up to meet me, and I tried clumsily to tuck and roll. I landed on a rock with a solid thump.

"I told you to come down before it wore off," Joey made a mark in his notebook.

"Why didn't I get to fly!" Tanner was too indignant to care that I'd fallen.

Ginger laughed a fair bit, although we couldn't hear it until her potion wore off too.

We all sat down for a minute and checked our supplies. Tanner was hungry so we all pulled out snacks too, and took little sips from our bottles.

Joey didn't trip until we stood up to put our packs back on. He misjudged the weight, and was off balance when he stood up. He stumbled backwards.

I screamed and leapt forward to catch him, but I was too slow or too far away.

He toppled off the edge.

I scrambled over to the lip of the gorge, lying down flat so I wouldn't fall over too.

Joey hadn't fallen all the way to the bottom, instead hitting a ledge halfway down. He lay on his pack, crumpled and bent all out of shape. If the position of his limbs wasn't enough of an indicator, the crimson that was spreading steadily from his head was.

"What happened?" Ginger asked, her voice quaking. Her back had been turned, and I was grateful at least that she hadn't seen Joey fall.

"Joey tripped," I whispered.

Since the actual death was over, the next step was the revival. We'd been given rope, but we'd put it all in Joey's pack, as he was the most responsible and least likely to lose it. As that was the case, we'd have to climb down to Joey, and climb back up, without any extra safety. Tanner insisted I wasn't allowed to do anything because I could die and then Joey would be really dead too.

Ginger didn't have any of the matter-confusion potion left, but she dug out a potent agility potion. After threatening to kill Tanner myself, I took the potion and climbed down the wall.

I carried another of the agility potions with me, so Joey could make the climb back up.

As I descended, taking twice as much time as was necessary, I remembered what the King had said about my involvement in the mission. Teenagers are stupid.

Joey wasn't yet in the full throws of rigor mortis, although his body was already stiffening. I had to tug to get his arms back into place, and his legs were even harder. I made sure his spinal column was more or less straight, then I held his hand.

I'd touched him plenty to rearrange his body, but only when I intended to bring him back did he revive.

He made the mistake of jolting upright.

"What…" he was out of breath, his eyes wide with terror.

"How're you doing Joey?" I tried to keep my voice light and friendly.

"I just…" he patted his chest, and raised his hands in front of him to check that all his fingers were intact.

"Don't worry, you didn't lose any of your notebooks. Although there might be some blood on that one. Oops."

An unhealthy pallor had stolen over his face, "I just died, didn't I?"

My gut curled in on itself. His tone was so despondent, so terribly unlike his normal undaunted voice.

"Are you ok Joey?"

He didn't seem to hear me, looking toward the gorge. As soon as he looked down he bent over and vomited.

"I don't think he's ready to climb back up," Tanner offered helpfully.

"Climb…you want me to climb back up?" Joey wiped sick off his face.

"Whenever you feel up to it," I said, suddenly worried that I should've brought another potion for when mine ran out. I hadn't expected to need it, Tanner's revivals went so fast, and he was always impatient to move after he'd been waken. I'd always assumed it was to prove to himself that he was alive.

"I'm sorry Kennedy, I don't know if I can do it," He looked over the edge again. He didn't vomit this time, but the green in his face increased.

"Uh…" My mind ran through a few dozen different scenarios, trying to find one that would get Joey and I out of here without too many injuries.

Joey shook his head and stood up, "No. That's irrational. I'll be fine if I take the potion."

He carefully lifted his backpack onto his shoulders, and the straps left red smears up his arms.

"Joey, you're not well. I won't let you climb until you really

94

feel up to it.”

“No, I’m fine,” Joey held out his hand for the bottle.

“Nope. You’re not. Sit down.”

Joey finally leveled his eyes at me, “I’m fine. Give me the bottle.”

“Don’t give it to him,” Ginger called.

Joey glared at me for a minute more, then finally relented. He shrugged the bag off his shoulders and squatted down.

“We should send our packs up with your rope,” I suggested.

“Let me find it...” Joey reached into his bag, and dug around for a second.

The rope was thick but stringy. We tied one end to a rock and looped the other into the straps of his bag.

After a few attempts we got the rock up to Ginger and Tanner. They hoisted the bag up, then tossed the rope back down, and suggested that Joey tie it around his waist.

It was much too small to actually secure him, and he must’ve known that, but he tied it around nevertheless.

I handed him the potion wordlessly and he downed it in one swig. He threw the bottle down aggressively, and seemed to take strength from the way it shattered. He noticed me watching him, and threw himself up the wall.

I climbed much more cautiously, especially when I felt my agility wearing off. The handholds that had seemed so easy to scramble down became treacherous. I couldn’t risk too big of a stretch and slip on a mossy stone.

When I reached the top Tanner grabbed my hands and hauled

me over.

"You couldn't have gone any faster?"

"I enjoy bothering you too much for that."

Joey was standing ten feet from the cliff edge, and shaking. His usually impeccable posture was missing, and for a second I was terrified I'd left his spine bent out of place. A split second later I realized what I should've realized the second I brought him back.

The psychological trauma. The trauma I'd always assumed was healed along with the bodily injuries. Joey hadn't been healed of it, he was shaking like a leaf.

Ginger had a hand on his shoulder, and was trying to comfort him. I wanted to say something, but I knew she had it covered.

Tanner's expression changed to one of concern when I turned on him.

"You told me you didn't remember dying," I poked him hard in the chest.

Tanner stumbled back in surprise, "Calm down Edy, I just–"

"Just what! Just what Tanner! You thought you'd keep this little thing a secret huh?"

"Kennedy–" Tanner kept walking backwards, and I kept walking forward.

"Do you remember every time you died?" I was shouting, but the words were muffled in my head, like they were coming from great distances.

"Yes. I didn't want you–" Tanner tripped backwards over a root, and landed on his butt in the dirt.

"Don't you dare say it was for me. Don't you dare!" I wasn't shouting, my voice had taken on the grating quality of a rockfall.

Tanner stood up, and I hated the way I had to look up to meet his eyes when he said, "It didn't matter so I didn't want to bother you with it."

He was angry now too, and seeing my rage mirrored on his face reminded me that I wasn't really angry.

I looked away and after a brief pause I asked, "Is that why you're afraid of rivers? Is it because you drowned?"

That had been his first death. And the worst, in my opinion. A small offshoot of Befreiung der Verdammten had tied his hands behind his back after he'd stolen jewels from them, and tossed him into the river.

It had taken me three days to find him washed up along the shore. It was only my second resurrection. I hadn't even known if it would work. Still, I'd lined him up as best I could, and I'd breathed life back into him.

He'd sat up coughing water from his lungs, while his fish-eaten skin had still been fitting itself together.

"Yes. But it didn't matter because I was alive!"

My jaw clenched, "You should've told me."

Tanner's biggest phobia was my fault. No doubt my father's agoraphobia was my fault too. The realization felt as though my chest was concaving, my ribs digging uncomfortably into my heart.

Tanner threw up his arms in annoyance, "It wouldn't change anything! I didn't want you to worry over nothing."

"It would've changed things. I would've tried to keep you

from dying more."

"Please! We took those risks for good reasons! We kept ourselves alive! We paid off your family's debts!"

I turned to him, and I could feel a fire alight in my eyes, "My family could have managed. I would've happily lived in the slums if I'd known!"

Tanner opened his mouth to say something, but I wasn't done.

"When you said you weren't afraid of dying anymore you were lying."

"Oh really?" Tanner's angry laugh contorted his face in a way I hadn't seen before.

"You aren't afraid of death, but you're afraid of dying. If you weren't you'd be fine with the river."

Tanner started shouting, but I shouted over him.

"And the poison? We completely ignored you as you died! You were suffering, but I thought you wouldn't remember! We could've put you out of your misery! We could've done something!"

"I said I didn't care! It didn't matter as long as I was alive! Don't tell me what I'm afraid of!" Tanner was breathing hard. Maybe all the anger I felt at myself was making me hunch, but Tanner seemed as large as the Northerner in that moment. He towered over me, anger crackling like lightning in the air.

Words were clogging in my throat, all vying to be the first out of my mouth. I don't want you to be afraid. Cloying. You should've trusted me enough to tell me. Revealing. I'm sorry I was selfish. Honest.

I swallowed them down and turned on my heel, walking back to where we'd dropped the packs.

We wouldn't be going any further today.

I stomped around camp finding the biggest rocks I could carry to make a tall fire ring. I relieved the pressure in my head by kicking them into a circle.

Tanner stood alone where I'd left him for a minute before joining Ginger and Joey.

Ginger tried to talk to me once, but I told her I just needed to think, and she knew the look I gave her enough that she gave me space.

After we'd all eaten I laid on my back on the dirt.

The thoughts I'd been trying so hard to keep from sinking in all hit me, and I tried to keep tears from springing to my eyes.

All the times we'd laid dangerous traps that got Tanner killed came back with awful clarity. We could've stayed pickpockets. Of course he'd been the one to suggest moving on to bigger and better things when he knew I could revive him, but I should've said no. We could've gotten along fine.

Memories of another revival pressed down on my chest. These were memories I'd tried much harder to suppress for a much longer time. I kept my eyes open, hoping the visions couldn't penetrate my imagination that way. They attacked every time I blinked. I saw the shovel coming down. I saw the attacker, for just a brief second as they turned to face me. Then I remembered the red. The way it pooled around–

"I want to thank you Kennedy," Joey interrupted my thoughts as he sat heavily beside me.

I shook my head sharply, "Don't thank me Joey."

"No Kennedy, I need to. If it weren't for you...Just accept my thanks please?"

I nodded, but my hands were clenched into fists on my stomach.

"Was it" I paused to try and stop my voice from shaking, "Was it horrible?"

I didn't want to open my eyes, but I peered through my eyelashes at Joey.

The light played across his face, and in every flicker it cast his expression differently. Finally, almost imperceptibly, Joey nodded.

A sob rose in my throat. Before I could let it out I hopped to my feet and tried to walk away from the fire.

The number of times I'd teased Tanner about dying seemed so crass and tactless. How had I not seen his fear? The answer was obvious. Like the stolen objects he hid so jealously, it was because Tanner wanted certain parts of him to be known only by the bards who told his story.

Before I got too many steps away I heard a familiar tread tailing me. I sighed, and let my head fall. I tried to release all my emotions in a single breath. I didn't want them all to come out when I tried to talk.

Tanner came up beside me, and he no longer seemed so huge.

"I'm sorry I yelled at you," I mutter. I sound just like my sisters, the way they apologize as if saying sorry was some great shame.

I raised my head and turned to face him straight on, "I'm sorry I yelled at you, and I'm sorry you've been through so much because of me."

Tanner shrugged.

"Really. I'm sorry."

Tanner scratched the back of his neck, "Apology accepted. And I guess I'm sorry I didn't tell you that I remembered it."

"No, don't apologize for that. I had no right to be angry because–"

"Shut up Edy, you're starting to sound like Joey. We're even. You're sorry, I'm sorry. Don't make this all weird and sappy."

I laughed, and the sob in my throat melted back into my lungs like hot wax, "Sounds good."

We had to cross two more bridges before we reached the next town. Luckily both were the ones I'd originally pictured, with rotting boards linking the bottom ropes. Joey still clipped himself in, and Ginger gave him special potions to drink, and we got over without too many problems.

After we crossed each one we'd keep walking for thirty feet or so before we dropped off our packs though, just in case.

None of us died in the intermediate time, although Ginger passed out from dehydration once. She'd been drinking potions so much she'd forgotten to drink water. After a few hours we started on our way again.

When we came to the town, we met with another new agent of Kingsman.

This town didn't have a tavern, so we met at the Inn. The Innkeeper greeted us with a hand extended as if he expected payment before he'd even speak. He was a tall man with skin like old leather, and dozens of glittering earrings. It gave him a distinctly eccentric appearance.

When we said we were looking for Kingsman's agent, the Innkeeper dismissed us with a wave of the hand. After a brief second of panic, someone tapped me on the shoulder.

The agent looked like he'd been hit with a hammer when he was little. It wasn't just that he was squat, although he certainly was, it was the odd way he was squat. His head seemed to have been squished down into his shoulders, and his pelvis seemed to have been rammed into his ribcage.

He explained that the Pied Piper–or the instrumental witch as Joey nicknamed him–had moved at an unexpectedly quick pace, and his army was approaching. The piper–witch–apparently had a small primary group that accompanied him at the head of the party, and they all stayed in the Inns along the way. If innkeepers didn't let him in, he made them.

Ginger asked if any more fleeing kids had been found, and the agent explained that the children took a harsher route through the mountains to avoid the rope bridges, but that groups were continually stopping in to beg what they could from the villagers.

The agent said it would be best if we remained in town and set up defenses. He explained that a small army was gathering to

102

fight the Piper should the need arise, but they'd be hiding in the caves until we gave the all clear.

We had a quick tete-a-tete, and all agreed it made sense. Ginger was happy because she could commandeer part of the kitchen to prepare some of the draughts she'd been running low on. Tanner was happy because he could sleep in a bed while we waited. Joey was happy because he could catch up on the reading he'd missed, and particularly because we wouldn't have to cross any more bridges.

I was extremely excited. The agent had mentioned that many of the Red Rebellion's traps were nearby, and I couldn't wait to see them in person, maybe take them apart and put them back together better.

All in all, we were hopeful. We'd made it to a village indistinguishable from any other along the trail, but it felt like a final destination.. We were somewhere, at least. Somewhere we could plan to make a difference—somewhere we could complete our mission and be freed by the King.

If we'd paused to think about the situation, we'd have realized just how daunting it was to stop an army, just how scary it was to not know when they'd be arriving, but we didn't pause to think.

We ran on artificial certainty right up until the army found us.

Chapter 8
Fitz

The rich corridors of the autumnal oaks gave way to flat seas of pale grass, then to hills of scraggly plants. Everything seemed more vibrant than usual while I traveled with my army. We passed all manner of quaint homesteads and villages.

There was a startling opposition between the reactions people had to our passage.

Sometimes they scattered, leaving tables set for dinner, and food burning in the ovens. I checked most of the houses at first, then I found more and more people willing to obey my commands without the use of my flute. They made it much more efficient to look through the town. They turned off stoves, put out fires, and let out the animals. I kept a pack of dogs for a minute, but they were harder to control, after a few minutes without music, they reverted to their natural wildness.

The others stayed in their homes. They turned out the lights and blocked the doors, and only whispered and shushed each

other when we knocked at their doors. I gave them a special treat.
Daemon would break the windows, and I played my melodies
through the broken glass, until they swarmed up from their
basements and from under the bed to open the door and join the
swelling crowd.

Gradually my music got better as well. The notes cracked
less, my fingers became more confident in their holds.

The army followed at my back, moving in sync until their
collective footsteps sounded like the walking of a giant. Picturing
them that way made it even easier to manage them. Instead of
picturing a hundred faces in a crowd, I could imagine a single
monster, its skin a patchwork of hundreds of others.

When I became tired, it wasn't because of the searching.
That was enthralling, seeing so many lives reflected in the
furniture of so many neat, loved, lived in homes. Occasionally,
when there was no Inn, I chose a house and stayed the night.

The halls had none of the nail marks and angry dents the
orphanage had. Some had little bowls of candy set on the tables,
laid out with care for anyone who passed. I plunked a few keys on
pianos, and plucked the strings of the round bodied instruments. I
curled up under the colorful sheets the children used, and imagined
I lived there. I wished the people who wore the clothes in those
closets would come in and tuck the sheets tighter under my chin.

That's what exhausted me. The constant imagining of better
things and loving people. Everytime I woke up, it was to a devoted
but empty family, and a band of people whose loyalty was only
as sure as the penny whistle against my lips. It felt like the day

after the Summer festival, when all the fair skinned children were missing, and the much diminished group, the shadows, were all assigned new beds. It was a once-a-year reminder of just how many others could be loved, while we were consistently passed over.

It had become a daily reminder. Even staying in the Inns brought up the pain anew, because as I came down the crooked stairs or walked the worn halls, I could hear tavern songs and merriment echoing from cobwebbed corners of the building. No one in my army sang, unless I asked them too. Music wasn't the same when it was forced.

In the end, I let Daemon and the awake followers lead the army. The snake had asked if he could be given the power to control the army in my absence. I'd granted it with a bored wave, and a thought.

The snake slipped out from between my fingers, and made its way up to my arm, tightening like a bracer. I didn't pay it much heed. If it got to close to my neck, I'd cut off its head. I would be King, afterall.

Except that too had lost its savor. Please don't look down on me reader, I wanted the love a King had. The veneration and adoration of a kingdom. Daemon made it remarkably clear the King was not always loved. He talked of his Red Rebellion proudly, proclaiming his hatred for the hypocrisies of our leader. In quieter tones he whispered of his new rebellion.

He still wore his purple tunic, and when he spoke of his rebellion he muttered of the color, held it in revere as if the color

106

itself made a man a hero. I suggested he call his new effort the Purple Putsch, but he shook his head, and urged me to speak in quieter tones.

In his nasally voice he explained that the color was determined after its success or failure. The Red Rebellion was only considered such because the blood spilt stained the earth red.

That idea made my blood cower in my veins.

It was when we passed one of the battle sites that I left the group. The earth was indeed stained red. It looked as if mother earth herself was bleeding because of how far along the horizon the crimson stretched.

Daemon had failed to mention the state they'd left the battleground in. Bodies had been stacked on top of each other, and covered in the thinnest layer of dirt. In places noses, toes, fingers, and sometimes entire limbs, poked out of the dirt. That's what I imagined at least, to make it less gruesome. In truth–dare I say–it was much worse.

Burrowing bugs and all kinds of rodents had been feasting for years. The bones of the long dead stuck through the mud like skeletal trees. From a distance they seemed to be rows of crop. We had to be careful where we stepped, lest we break through a ribcage and sink into the carnage.

I played a tune, and the insects dug deeper into the ground and didn't disturb our passing. The rodents scurried off, although I'm not entirely sure where I sent them. In their passing the silver glint of the soldiers breastplates were revealed.

These bodies were those of men and women who'd loved

the King. They'd served him, and it had done them no good. Their devotion was nearly as blind as those who followed my whistle.

So I told Daemon to continue on. I found a cozy homestead, waltzed in the empty front room, stood at the balcony and imagined someone coming out to speak to me. A rat tried, and it really ruined the mood.

This family had no kids, and sleeping in a mattress as large as the parents seemed wrong. I stretched across one of the sofas, threw a lovingly knitted blanket over my toes, and fell asleep.

I dreamt my head was thrown back, as if in utter devotion to some prophet. Yellowed bone fingers lowered snakes onto my face, and they slithered down my throat, filling it with their thrashing. When they reached my stomach they gnawed their way through, to find I was hollow. They began to fill the chasm inside me, twisting in and out of my ribs. They had purple gemstones for eyes, and when worms and rats ate through my skin, the light glinted off the gemstones and made my insides glitter.

Chapter 9
Kennedy

Kingsman's agent woke us by barging into our room, waving his pudgy arms about as quickly as he could.

Ginger and I were ready in under a minute, as were Joey and Tanner (well Tanner hadn't done his usual morning hair ritual, but other than that).

We passed through a small alley and into the neighboring shop. The agent stuffed wads of cotton into his ears, and watched avidly out the front window for the approach of the army. Personally, I didn't think we'd miss the army, but Kingsman's man had less trust.

My traps were arranged, Ginger had distributed her vials, Tanner had his strength ring and a sword unwisely gifted to him, and Joey had refreshed us on the plan.

The advance group, with the instrumental witch and his most devoted followers would check every building until they reached the Inn. We'd rigged a series of minor traps in those homes, traps that would look like accidents: boards on the second floor that would fall through when weight was placed on them, moldings above the doors that would slip down to conk the heads of unsuspecting visitors et cetera.

When they reached the Inn they'd pause for the night, leaving us safe, as we were one house down from there. The Innkeeper was prepared to be fully cooperative, and offer them specific rooms on the second floor. He would light a candle in the third floor window if he was still in full control of himself, and two candles if something was more dangerous than he suspected. He would only light them after the group had settled in for the night.

Manually triggered traps were sewn into the rooms, so when they were asleep we'd go in and pull a few strings. Hopefully scent potions would be smashed, releasing sleep potions that would knock out the group. Ginger, Tanner, and Joey would head up the stairs with their personal arsonals to make sure the witch and his followers were really knocked out, and they'd be tied up. The witch would be treated to a special sleep ointment Ginger concocted that should keep him out the entire trip back to the capital. We'd have to tip nutrient rich smoothies down his throat to keep him alive, but once we made it back to the capital the King would decide what to do with him.

We'd even made a stretcher we could attach to the rope bridges with our clips to get him across.

We were about as confident as we could be. Joey, of course, had made seven separate lists of things that could go wrong and eight lists of responses to those things. Tanner had his devil-may-care attitude, and the plan to overuse his supposedly enhanced strength. Ginger was bouncing with adrenaline, and nearly dropped her potions with all the jostling.

I was feeling a little left out. I'd been busy with the rest of them in preparations, but now I felt like I had no part. That was by design, but I didn't like it nonetheless.

Our past experiences should've taught us something, but we were still somewhat surprised when everything started to go wrong from the get-go.

When the group came into view, they passed completely by all the houses we'd rigged, only peeking in the windows. It was an obvious break from the pattern, which was startling.

All our pent up energy started going the wrong direction. We pressed our faces up against the window, our breath fogged the surface until we could barely see.

Ginger really did drop one of her vials. Joey flipped furiously through the sixth of his eight lists, and started muttering a string of very creative and illustrative curses. Tanner's knuckles were white on the hilt of his sword. I squeezed the luck charm in my pocket, and rubbed a little circle in the fog so I could see.

We had a very small view of the main road, mainly because a mirror had been set up to allow us to see out. They figured a surreptitious mirror would be less suspicious than all of us out on the deck, watching as they approached.

"I think they're going to the Inn," Tanner breathed.

"That general direction at least…" Ginger replied, dropping her bottle a second time.

"Keep that up and you'll put us to sleep," Tanner scoffed.

Ginger rolled her eyes, but tucked the vial into her belt.

"They may be checking in early, and scan the houses later. We can wait for the sign to go. They could also be trying to hasten the journey, and skip both the searches and the stay at the Inn, but that seems unlikely, as the army is a full three days behind."

"So we should wing it?" Tanner's voice was just a little too eager.

"Absolutely not," Joey whispered at the same time Ginger said, "Sounds good to me."

"My vote counts twice because I'm the smart one," Joey muttered, "Kennedy the final decision is up to you."

"Let's see if they're going to the Inn. We can decide afterward."

Someone tapped me on the shoulder and I leapt into action. I spun about, raising my fist. My alarm triggered Tanner to free his sword and wave it dramatically, in a similar stance to my own. Ginger spun around too, her hands reaching to her belt. Joey didn't even notice.

The agent of Kingsman jolted back at our terrified response.

"Something is off here. I don't think the necromancer should go in with you. I can trigger all the traps when the time comes, and then we're all insured in case something goes wrong."

I opened my mouth to argue, but that would be pointless. He had way too much cotton in his ears to pick up on anything I said.

I turned back to the window so he couldn't see my mouth moving, "I am not staying here."

112

"He does make a good point though," Joey offered unhelpfully.

"I'm sorry Kennedy, but it's true. You're not that good at hand to hand combat anyway," Ginger spoke to me in the quiet, sweet voice she sometimes used on her pet toads.

"We got this Edy, you don't need to come."

Their combined discouragement and the use of that irritating nickname made me fume. I understood where they were coming from, sure, but I was still pissed I couldn't do anything.

"Let's just see what happens, huh?" I kept my voice monotone, but I saw Ginger and Joey exchange a knowing look, and it made me bristle.

By the time we all were back at the window, the fog from our noses had faded. We had a very clear view of the troop entering the Inn.

We took turns watching to see if they left again, but slowly noon-day faded into dusk, then into the sapphire shades of early night.

I was dozing off on the armchair when Ginger exclaimed.

"They put one light up!"

"You sure there aren't two?" Tanner stepped over to peer at the mirror.

"Of course I'm sure, you idiot. I have eyes."

"Time to go then," Joey said, cutting Tanner off before he could say anything particularly snippity.

I stood up, all my drowsiness evaporating.

"It's only one candle so I'm coming," I stood up and shook

my feet to wake my sleepy legs.

They all hesitated, all frozen in their stances. It was comedic really.

Joey sighed, "I suppose that's fair. But stay back and run if we say to."

"Brilliant plan Sherlock."

We filed out through the back, and entered the inn through a side door that had purposefully been left unlocked and slightly open. Tanner went first, his sword raised in an unsteady offensive posture.

The door swung in on well oiled hinges without a sound. Dying candles lit the way to the front room and the upper floors. Tanner, Joey, and Ginger all crept down that hall, stepping as quietly as possible.

I stole one of the candles and walked down a different hallway. The old boards were scuffed and uneven under my feet, but soon enough I'd reached the storage room.

That door was as quiet as the first, and I stepped through into a kind of heaven. Barrels of salted meat and dried fruit were stacked along the walls, accompanied by all kinds of mysterious powders. They were labeled, so I suppose not all that mysterious, but the Innkeeper's handwriting was illegible.

The most exciting part were the strings that hung from the ceiling like cobwebs. They were thin, mostly, and made of clear fishing thread or embroidery floss. It had taken some doing, but we'd strung them through the entire house. All I needed to do was tug on the end, where we'd hung all kinds of baubles, and

114

somewhere above, a little potion would drop, putting the piper and his cronies to sleep, if they weren't already.

The wires hung limply down, dangling like the cut strings of a marionette. I brushed my fingers over the small baubles. There was the clay heart for the fifth room, here the golden clasp for room seven.

There were twelve rooms total, and knocking out the posse would be as simple as tugging on the baubles. Except…the string hung limp…I raised my candle.

A cannon ball settled in my stomach.

I pulled the clasp, and didn't stop pulling until I had meters of wound string tangled in my hand and on the floor.

The end whipped out of the small hole and slipped through my fingers.

Someone had cut the end. I tried the clay heart, for the same result. My heart beat an uneven rhythm in my chest. Someone had snipped the wires.

Hot wax dripped onto my fingers, and I stole one of Joey's curses as I dropped the candle. I didn't stoop to pick it up as the end was snuffed against the carpet.

I threw the door open and shot into the hall. My footsteps weren't stealthy but it didn't matter.

This was a trap. Someone had set us up, but who? Kingsman's agent? He had no time. One of the army? They didn't know what we were planning.

I sprinted around a corner, and was immediately clotheslined by a section of the same fishing wire I'd used for my traps.

I was thrown onto my back, and all of the breath was knocked from my lungs. I gaped like a fish on land, and tried to push myself up.

A boot landed on my chest and held me firmly down.

"I told them I'd end you. They didn't believe I could," The Innkeeper's voice was a rasp.

End. He'd said end.

"Befreiung der Verdammten," I spat, wondering where he'd hidden his gemstones.

"Yes little pythoness, I am an Eternal One," He pulled a knife from his belt.

I bucked suddenly, knocking him off balance. I rolled out from under his foot, and used the wall to help me up.

The man growled like a wild thing and leapt at me. His knife flashed toward my chest, but I raised my foot and kicked him back.

He threw his knife, and it lodged in the paneling behind me. I gripped it in my fist.

He shifted his weight, and I saw what I hadn't before.

The earrings I'd only noticed for their quantity were violet.

I should've realized. Why hadn't I realized?

He tackled me, his lithe arms wrapping around my torso and trapping my hands against my sides. I contorted my arm just enough to tickle his side with the blade before I was trapped against the floor.

The knife clattered out of my hands, and the man knelt over me. His fist came down hard, and heard a loud crack and felt a burst of pain.

116

I raised my hands to block his next blow but he moved right through them. I closed my eyes as his fist came down, and one of them popped red when his fist hit.

The next time he raised his hand I caught his arm and pulled it down.

He fell forward, and I head-butted him.

In his momentary disorientation I scrambled for the knife. I held it in front of me with both hands like it was a sword.

The Innkeeper stepped back, one hand holding his side where I'd nicked him. The blood was black in the dark, and it bubbled between his fingers.

Still, he grinned, "Your poor friends are probably already ended."

I raced at him. He tried to dodge back, but I impaled him on the knife. His eyes bulged as the knife twisted into his gut.

He stumbled backwards, and I went with him, carried by my momentum. The knife pinned him to the floor when he hit.

"I'll get you next time," he groaned, and when he smiled, blood stained his teeth.

I pulled out the knife and stabbed down once, severing his glittering ear from his head with one strike.

The man screamed, and it was a sound like I'd never heard before.

I stood up and stumbled away from the gurgling man.

Only then did I hear Tanner shouting.

I pulled the knife from the floorboards and started running, trying my utter best not to look at what I'd done.

I tripped on a wrinkled carpet and ran into the wall at the bottom of the stairs. I coughed and turned toward the staircase.

I had imagined my friends silhouetted at the top, swords flashing, potion's glittering. Instead I saw the crumpled form of a person lying against the banister.

It wasn't anyone I recognized, thank heavens.

I crawled up the last few steps, peeking just over the lip of the top stair so hopefully no one would see me.

Ginger and Tanner were against the back wall, farthest from the staircase. Three burly men were bearing down on them, trying to block Tanner's sword with their short knives and dodging everytime Ginger lobbed a vial.

Joey was backing through an open doorway, his épée flashing in the light. Two men were forcing him back.

They all wore tunics died purple, although some were seeping with crimson. Besides the man curled up on the stairs, there were three men limp against the walls. One was breathing shallowly, blood leaking from a wound in his stomach. A second's throat had been slashed, the thin even cut more likely the handiwork of Joey than Tanner. The third's skin was scratched raw, and his eyes bulged out of his sockets.

Scarlet sprayed against the wall in scattered droplets. Tanner's hand was dripping with it, as was a cut above Ginger's eyebrow.

I took this all in before I even heard a sound. The adrenaline and the sight had occupied every ounce of brainpower. As soon as I heard the screech of metal on metal and the screaming though, I wished I hadn't.

It echoed around me in a discordant cacophony, the sounds seemed to make everything a darker shade of terror.

"--an ambush! Get the army! The Piper's not here!" Tanner was yelling, and I didn't realize until later that he was talking to me.

I darted forward, running into the first room on my left. I found the sleep potion, and pivoted to leave the room.

One of the men stood blocking my path.

"I thought the Innkeeper'd take care of ya, ah well," the knife the man held was no larger than mine.

I threw the potion at his chest. I would've aimed for his head, but that would've been easier to dodge.

It broke against him, and the wetness left a circle on his shirt.

He looked down, as if checking to see if it was blood he felt dripping down his stomach. As he did his eyelids slipped closed, and he slumped heavily to the floor.

I sprinted out of the room, covering my mouth so I wouldn't pass out.

I hurdled the heap of a man, and stood in the center of the hallway.

Joey had been pushed into the room, but the second of his attackers had fallen against the wall, blood spilling from his side. Tanner had dropped his sword, and blood was spilling from his hand, perhaps it had been sliced.

"Get out of here!" Tanner roared, "It's an ambush."

This time I understood that he was talking to me. Except I

couldn't run. These men were part of Befreiung der Verdammten. They knew what I could do. They might burn my friends bodies. They could take them apart and keep the pieces. I didn't know, but I knew it would be bad.

Some of them turned around when Tanner's eyes had caught on me, and now two of them advanced on me.

"That your blood?" One man asked, smirking at my hands.

I didn't answer, instead I sprung forward, swinging wildly at his head.

The tall man ducked lazily out of the way, and swiped at my side. I didn't care, I'd just wanted him out of the way.

I passed him and ran into the room Joey had been backed into.

The man had Joey in a corner. I stabbed him in the back. The man cried out, and dropped his knife, his back arching in pain. Joey thunked the man on the head, and he collapsed to the floor.

Joey wiped his face with a shaking hand, "What are you doing here?"

"I wanted to warn you about the ambush."

Joey speared his blade forward, just over my shoulder, "A little late for that."

I turned around and found that Joey had stabbed a tall man who'd crept up behind me.

I rolled to the ground as the man swung at me, and Joey stabbed again.

Ginger screamed, and I ducked past the man back into the hallway. Tanner was a puddle on the floor, the attacker had Ginger

120

by her hair, holding his knife to slice her throat.

I threw my knife at him. The hilt hit the man in the shoulder, doing nothing more than startling him. He moved his arm away from Ginger's neck to hold me off.

The pause was enough time for me to push forward, and I caught the man's raised arm in mine. He released Ginger's hair and dropped his knife into the other hand. He stabbed my side, and I screamed and wrenched away. I took the knife with me.

His was longer than the one I'd had before. I raised it in front of me to ward the man off. I tried not to think about the blood–my blood–that coated the blade and dripped onto my fingers.

Ginger was sobbing dryly, her hands over her neck, where a thin red line was etched into her skin.

"You're good for a bunch of kids," the man snickered, "but you haven't ended anyone today."

I waved the knife threateningly.

Ginger grabbed the leg of my pants, "Bring Tanner back," she rasped, "bring him back and he'll stop the fight."

"He's not dead," I replied, kicking out sharply at the man bearing down on me.

There was a thump from the other room, and the man emerged, clutching Joey's sword.

Ginger, Tanner, and I, were bunched up against the wall opposite the staircase. The two men were standing menacingly, shoulder to shoulder, filling the entire hallway with their bulk.

My puny knife seemed to shrink when faced with them.

A nasally voice came from behind them, "Step aside."

The men shrank back, and allowed us the sight of a small man.

His face was odd, his broad nose stood out on his face, his eyes were little slits, and his mouth seemed to be a lipless slice across his entire face, which literally stretched ear to ear when he smiled.

"So you're the unholy monster they sent," he looked me up and down.

Ginger tugged on my pants again, "We need him right now."

I glanced down at Tanner. His face was sallow, but he was still breathing shallowly.

"You killed a surprising number of my men," he looked at the blood splattered walls, and his soldiers folded against them like crumpled clothing.

"I suppose the kings not a complete fool," he shrugged, "then again, he lets us all suffer in poverty while he lives lavishly."

Ginger was fingering her belt like she'd find more potions there.

The nasally man took another step forward. He was apparently unarmed, but he didn't shrink from my knife, "I'm sorry, already talking politics. I suppose I ought to introduce myself. I'm Daemon."

The name was awfully familiar, "Daemon? Daemon John?"

The man smiled again, and listed his head to the side, "You know me?"

I took a small step backwards, my ankles pressing into

Tanner's arm.

"You're the trap maker," I said, trying to remember what Joey had said, "the leader of the Red Rebellion."

"It's true I began that war, but it had been building for some time. As for the traps, I'm rather good at making them. Even this one worked out well."

I shrugged, "I don't know, it didn't seem all that clever. Cut a few wires, kill a few kids. Anyone could do that."

Ginger wiped the sweat from her face and tried to stand. She leaned heavily against the wall.

The broad-nosed man's smile twisted, "you're goading me, but I suppose I'll relent. This isn't the only trap that's being sprung."

I muttered something under my breath and Ginger sat back down.

The nasally man took another step forward, and the other men stood behind him menacingly. Arrogance seeped from every pore. His eyes seemed to say, you are mine. You will not escape.

"You should help us. We've had a lot of…unfortunate mishaps over the years. Those of the faith have come back, of course, but not everyone believes."

I shook my head.

The man rolled his eyes, "We aren't the bad guys here. You're here killing all my people, trying to stop an army from marching to stop a tyrant. A tyrant, I might add, who is using children protect himself. Tell me, who's in the wrong?"

The words tried to worm their way into my head, but I shook

them out my ears.

"The army isn't working of their own free will."

"How do you know?"

Ginger tugged on my pant leg. I knew that was the signal.

I kicked out, planting my boot in the stomach of Daemon John and sending him into the men behind him, who both tripped over themselves to catch him.

Then I reached back and dropped my knife. Just like his story with the merchant, the fallen knife killed Tanner.

My ankle, still pressed to his side, was all it took to bring him back. His skin stitched itself together around the knife, until he was well enough to pull it from his own neck, and watch as the hole fixed itself.

The transition from life to death and back to life was so fast Tanner could move immediately.

He started to say something, but one of the men was already advancing on me, so I didn't have time to listen.

I swung around and stepped behind the man, kicking him in the backside and sending him sprawling. Tanner slammed the butt of the knife into the back of his skull and knocked him flat.

The second man hit me with a backhand that twisted my neck sharply. I flew into the wall. Stars burst behind my eyes as my head pounded into the boards.

Tanner tried to stab the man in the stomach, but the knife was knocked from his hand.

Through my eyelashes I saw Ginger land a punch to the man's gut, only to be knocked to the ground.

124

The man kicked tanner backward into the wall as well, and I felt a cold certainty sink into my head.

This was it. I'd killed Tanner in a risky gamble, and it hadn't paid off. I should've run for the army. I should've realized the Innkeeper was a cultist. I shouldn't have taken this job. I shouldn't have tried to rob that wagon of the King's.

I groaned, and as I tried to move something slipped out of my pocket. My luck charm.

I reached for it, and it slipped between my fingers. They were slick with blood. Not just mine, although there was a fair amount of that.

It was kind of beautiful, really. The red seemed more vibrant than ever in the flickering candlelight.

Tanner stumbled to his feet, and the man raised a fist. Before he could attack, Tanner landed a punch. I almost laughed at him. It was such a weak punch. His elbow was bent all wrong, and his posture lended it no strength.

The man shot back, hitting the wall over the stairs with concussive force. A plume of plaster dust burst out around him, and then he fell onto the staircase, leaving a man sized imprint in the wall.

Tanner looked at his hand and understanding glinted in his eyes.

Shining on his index finger was the stolen strength ring.

Chapter 10
Kennedy

So, we didn't end up dead.

Tanner got Kingsman's agent, and explained the situation. There had been no sight of the piper, so he thought it was safe to come.

The army had medical kits prepared, and when Ginger had woken up, she brewed a few of her potions.

Joey had a severe headache and was rather sensitive to the light for a while. Tanner was physically fine, given his revival. Ginger was a little battered and bruised, and a little traumatized, but mostly ok.

They'd all been prepared for a little fighting. They'd expected it and been trained. Sure I'd had a day or two of practice at the palace, but not at the same level as they'd gotten.

As could be expected, I was the worst injured. I'd been stabbed in the side, my eye was black from the Innkeepers attacks, and my nose was slightly crooked from the same.

Almost worse were the visions that echoed in my head. I was a necromancer, a belated healer. I didn't kill people. I didn't injure people. Except I had.

I killed a man, stabbed another, and worse than the rest, I'd killed Tanner. My schemes had sometimes gotten him killed before, but this time had been different, I had literally been the one to end his life. I'd done it as a calculation, as a gamble, and I'd thought no more of it than a toss of the die. He wasn't a roll though, he wasn't an ace, he was a person, and I'd killed him.

All my friends were righteously exasperated at me for not getting out of there, but they held off beating on me too much because, unlike them, I was confined to the sickbed for a while. Then again, that 'while', was only as long as it took for Ginger to brew a healing potion.

Daemon John had escaped, but it didn't matter. I thought I understood his plan.

I only really figured it out when Joey agreed to discuss it with me.

He filled one of his empty notebooks with conclusions we drew from that first conversation, then the three after that.

For the sake of my sanity, I condensed the information. First, Daemon was still trying to overthrow the King, and he had a trap in motion. Second, both he and Befreiung der Verdammten had chosen purple as their color. The man who'd betrayed us was a member. The cult was the trap, and the members were closing in on the King like a noose. We already knew they could get into the palace. Third, the piper wasn't the type to take risks. He hadn't come because they'd known our attack would only involve children.

Under the circumstances, which we only explained the bare minimum of to the agent, we were told to return to the palace. It didn't matter that we hadn't caught the piper, we'd served our purpose.

We disagreed vehemently–we being Tanner and I–but the smartest of us thought it was for the best.

The piper would be reached through diplomatic means. They'd post reports that the piper could request almost anything in return for releasing the villagers. Honestly, I wasn't sure why they hadn't done that before sending a bunch of teenagers, but whatever, it was fine.

Once I'd taken enough time, and enough potion, to heal, the agent brought me to the Inn. The blood had been cleaned, all fallen weapons returned to their rightful owners–or perhaps the cleaners, it was impossible to tell–and all the dead were lined up neatly in the front room.

All the concussed or magicked enemies had already been taken into custody and started the long walk home. Since the dead couldn't walk, at least in my experience, the agent had been watching over the bodies until I was well enough to revive them.

The thick scent of supposedly holy herbs filled the room, and great pendants had been slung around the necks of the cultists, as if to keep their spirits from rising up.

I noticed, with a pang in my gut, someone had laid the Innkeepers ear next to his head.

The agent watched as I revived the men, one after another. They were already bound, so there was no struggle. A few of the men squirmed, and a few tried to speak through their gags, but no major problems there.

When I'd finished up, and was walking to leave, I noticed I'd healed the Innkeeper's ear on crooked. Ah well, at least it would be an interesting story should anyone ask.

The agent came by later as I was packing my bags, and he had one of the men in tow.

The squashed agent removed the man's gag, and the man cleared his throat.

I recognized the man as the one who had lain crumpled against the banisters. How had he died? Stabbed? Or was he the one with his throat slit?

"I did not become a spirit when I died," he paused and cleared his throat again, "so I have left Befreiung der Verdammten."

He raised his bound hands in front of him, and pooled in each of his palm were dozens of violet gemstones.

"I was one of the most devout followers," he explained, "if I did not come back, no one will."

He continued holding the gemstone out to me, and when I didn't react he cleared his throat for a third time, "I noticed you kept a luck stone. I wish you'd take these, as payment for bringing me back."

I scraped the stones from his palms, and was overwhelmed by the discordant mix of enchantments.

"Thank you," I said. I knew more words were due to him, but I had no idea what else to say. It didn't seem like the right time to insult his beliefs, and it seemed tactless to compliment him for leaving a foolish religion.

"No, thank you. Truly." With that he turned around, and was shuffled out of the room to join the rest of the prisoners on their walk.

I sat back on my bed and stared at the door. After a few minutes of confused contemplation I sighed and started sorting through the gemstones.

He had all the regular traits, devotion, strength, will, overpower, he had luck, and a bunch of traits I'd never seen before; greatness, pride, power, cleverness, beauty, and trusted. I couldn't identify all of the gemstones, so I tucked the rest into a separate pocket of my bag and hoped I'd remember to have Ginger's mother identify them.

We'd told the agent about Joey's accident, so instead of returning the way we'd come down Alte Straße, we were given instructions to follow the Unterer Flusspfad until we'd passed the gorges. He said it would be a longer walk, but if we had good enough timing, we could sneak onto a barge intended for the capital and ride most of the way there.

Tanner agreed to it, but I saw the apprehension in his face. I wasn't a huge fan of the idea either. If someone were to fall off the barge and drown, it could take weeks to find where they'd washed ashore.

Still, we took to the path the next day.

The first part was treacherous. Daemon's John had hundreds of traps along the road to Unterer Flusspfad, to discourage his men from retreating, and to keep any river men from joining the other side.

The river men were almost as notorious as northerners for their brutality, although theirs was less strange. They pulled the barges up the river. For decades donkeys and other beasts had pulled, but after livestock diseases, it became more economic for the burly men to pull the boats down the canal themselves. That being the case, they became giants, and the wild and illiterate way they spent their youth gave them vulgar manors and strange ideas of proper etiquette.

Joey held the trap map in his hands, and directed us through the most dangerous parts one at a time. Tanner stepped onto a triggered trap once, and just barely managed to dodge a spear that shot out of the ground, propelled by a shot of steam.

Ginger would go next, then Joey, leaving me for last. I would have to direct Joey myself, so if he died I'd have the map to get to him safely.

"Go straight for another few feet here," Joey prompted, and Ginger stepped cautiously forward.

"Ok, you went a little crooked there–" Joey muttered.

"What was that?" Ginger asked, "did you say something?"

"Nevermind!" Joey called, "just be careful here. Small step to your left."

Ginger stepped. The wrong way. A gasp squeezed from my lungs, but no spear launched from the ground.

"Ginger you stepped right," Joey said, "I need you to move very carefully to your left. Don't shift your weight too fast or you might trigger something."

I could only imagine the way the blood drained from her face. She clenched her fists at her side to keep her hands from shaking.

She shifted her left foot left, without ever picking it up off the ground.

It didn't matter. The slight movement had been enough.

The ground gave way beneath her, and she screamed with such raw terror I felt it myself.

"Ginger!" I screamed, uselessly. Tanner would have teased me for doing something so ineffectual, if it wasn't for the fact that it was over the death of my oldest friend.

I suppose it wasn't entirely a useless call, it drowned out Ginger's death scream.

Joey tried to keep his voice steady, "that's a spear pit. I'll walk with you until we get there, and I can…I can carry her down to where Tanner is, so we can lay her out."

I nodded, swallowing my tongue.

We moved slowly, more slowly than either Ginger or Tanner had. We made it safely though.

The pit was horrible. I looked at it, by accident, and immediately regretted it. I looked away, but I couldn't escape the sight tattooed into my retinas.

I was grateful, in a twisted way, that she'd fallen mostly vertically. It meant fewer spears had impaled her. Joey struggled pulling her out, the spears catching repeatedly inside her.

Tanner and Joey arranged her body, and when they stepped back, they wiped her blood off their hands and onto their shirts.

"Make sure she's all right," Tanner said, then corrected himself, "I don't mean alright. I mean that she's laid out entirely right." He cringed.

I just nodded. When I turned to look at Ginger my stomach dropped the same way it had when I'd found my first body.

Most deaths I healed were bloody. That's the nature of death. Not all blood is the same. The way it flows, the amount. The tissues, the way muscle and skin fold around the injuries. All of it illustrates a different picture.

Tanner's deaths were bloody, but in a composed way. The blood walked, instead of running. His skin sliced instead of tearing.

Joey's death had been bloody too, in a solid way. His blood had spilt, but not sprayed. The back of his head had been thick with scarlet, but there were no torn tissues or hanging skin to make it gory.

Ginger's death was horrific. The blood was draining from the soles of her feet, mixing with the dusty earth to create great globs of red mud. Her skin was ripped, broken open and uneven along the edges of the wounds.

I couldn't help but remember the gore of my first revival. It had been horrific too. Partially because it was emotionally brutal, but mainly because of the actual sight of it. I had been told to stay out of my Dad's work room, but I'd gone in, and broken the contraption he was making. He'd rushed to make an identical one, but it hadn't worked, and the buyer had beaten him to death for it. I'd been following Dad to say I was sorry, and I saw it all. The blood had splattered. The skin had shredded to mutilated pieces. His spine and his head weren't aligned.

I'd healed him wrong too. I didn't know I could revive him, so I'd just thrown myself at his attacker. The man had no qualms with killing my father, but he hesitated before he struck me. I scratched at his arms and I was thrown to the side before the man ran away. I crawled over to my father, and I tried to hold him together with my tiny fingers. He'd healed with his head on crooked. He never left the house after that.

I shook the thought away, and I squeezed my eyes shut as I crouched down. I still felt the blood soak through the knee of my pants.

I touched Ginger's hand, and shared whatever spark I held.

She came back screaming.

Chapter 11
The Piper

Daemon was restricted by his immovable humanness. He had to speak directly to the army for them to follow him.

I had the advantage of a telekinetic connection, but as I discovered when I woke in that old farmhouse, I was limited too. I only had control for as long as I was in view. Anytime I stepped over a hill or disappeared into the woods, I had to reestablish the connection with song before I had mental power over them again.

I would have searched for Daemon, and found him by following the trampled path of the army, but he came to find me.

He walked like his rib was broken, and spoke like his pride was too.

"There was an ambush at the Inn, it's lucky you weren't there."

I tightened the knitted blanket around my shoulders, "is that why you're alone?"

Daemon nodded, then tried to contort his expression into

something like regret.

The little snake was a coward then. He'd slithered away as soon as his friends started to fall.

"Were they working for the King? Is the King afraid?"

Daemon John smiled, his tongue tasting the air, "Of course he is afraid. Tyrants are always afraid of their subjects, that's why they oppress us so."

I may be stupid but please do not consider me a fool. When Daemon spoke of oppression, I recognized the irony. My immediate thought was the army I'd taken all will from.

The thought made my gut twinge, so I opened my mouth to prompt something that would make me feel better.

"How many men did they send to ambush us?"

Daemon hesitated, "Four…but one of them was a witch, and another was a necromancer."

"And what of the other two?"

"Swordsman. One of them had enchanted jewelry."

I was a threat worth four attackers. Maybe they were skilled, but it should have been more. Didn't they know how many people bowed before me? How large my army was?

"You said it was lucky I wasn't there," I pulled the knit blanket too tight around me and I felt like I was being suffocated, "but I think the opposite. If I had been there we'd have valuable additions to our army."

Daemon's tongue tasted the air again, "I don't think so. The King knows the limitations of your power. The witch, necromancer, and swordsman were all children. Your age, my liege."

That was offensive on two accounts. First, I was not a child. Second, four teenagers made up the King's entire offensive.

Strangely enough, my mind latched onto neither of the subjects.

"Were they familiar with one another?"

"They seemed like friends, yes."

A band of unusual teenagers foolhardily trying to stop a magical oppressor. It sounded like the stories we orphans had passed around like currency. Sometimes I could trade a good tale for an extra spoonful of soup, or a night with the best blanket.

The stories we told were of heroes and their triumphs. They came from humble origins, although all had loving parents. They earned love and respect from everyone for their gallantry, for their strength.

Perhaps I seem fickle–let me amend—it was fickle but that doesn't matter. At that moment I changed my objective.

I did not want to be King. I would be a tyrant, better men than Daemon would try to stop me.

"Where are they now?"

Something in Daemon's countenance changed as I said that, though I couldn't tell just what.

"I assume they're returning to the capital, why do you ask?"

"That should be of no importance to you," that sounded more kingly than heroic, so I tried again, "I only want to bring them to justice."

Daemon nodded, his eyes still squinted to slits, "What's your next move then, sire?"

I twirled the penny whistle between my fingers, "I will pursue them on foot. I don't think I'll be needing the army anymore, so I suppose I'd like you to return them."

"Prey tell, why is the army suddenly so superfluous?"

"It only takes one pipe to take over. Perhaps I'll make the king my puppet."

Snakes have many senses which people do not. I've heard stories of cobras that read intentions as clearly as text, and pythons who moved through the future and the past, leaving shed skins in every period they slipped through.

It wasn't too fanciful to assume Daemon had some of these abilities then, given how closely he related to the species.

"Shouldn't we retain the army? A backup measure, just in case?"

I shook my head, and raised my pipe to eye level. I peered at it as though inspecting the polish, but both Daemon and I knew that it was a barely veiled threat.

"I don't think it'll be necessary," I put the pipe back in my pocket, and stared Daemon down.

He was shorter than me, and while it wasn't by a great margin, I could look down my nose at him in a most pleasing way.

Yet, there was something in his expression that made me apprehensive. It could be the way his eyes had sunk so deep into his skull they were cast in shadow. It could be the way his lips were pursed, like he was keeping something wicked from slipping out alongside his tongue. It could be the way his nose was pulled up, like a wolf with its teeth bared.

No, more than any of those, it was the way he stood. His deportment was unnatural, somehow putting me in mind of demons and wild things.

"I'll be off then. Which way did you say they went?"

Ah, that's what it had been. Daemon's posture had been that of a rearing beast.

As I brushed past him to go on my way, his arm came out and wrapped around my throat.

He tightened his grip, and I found myself bending backwards and down. How had I let him get so close to me? A vein throbbed in his arm as I scrabbed uselessly against it.

"Can't whistle if you can't breathe huh?" He flexed and my mouth gaped open.

How had I forgotten the vision I had of him? Sinuous and scaly, trapping me tightly in coils like chains. His movements had been feather light, detectable only with real focus, and I'd been entirely too distracted.

I tried to grab my pipe, to spit any last air into it and stop this attack, but the penny whistle clattered from my pocket and out of reach.

"I was going to do this later, but you are really intent on ruining everything, aren't you. Did you really think anyone would love you just because you wore some stupid crown? Huh?"

His breath was hot against my ear, sending spiders running down my spine.

"Do you know what they call you? Pied Piper. Do you know

why?"

The spiders crept across my entire body, and I felt myself beginning to go limp. A few curious ones crawled across my eyes, blackening my vision. They skittered into my ears, filling them with scratching. I almost didn't hear Daemon's next words. Almost.

"Because that's all that anyone sees in you. Pied. Piper."

Daemon flexed again, and the spiders covered my eyes.

They followed me into my dreams too. Just like my previous nightmare, skeletal hands hovered over my face, my head was tipped back, and my mouth hung open. Instead of lowering snakes down my gullet, arachnids dripped from the bones. They danced their way down my throat, leaving their spun lace in great tangles. When my mouth was full of their unnatural crawling bodies, they began to cover my face, drowning me in webs until I couldn't so much as move as they ate through my skin.

Chapter 12
Kennedy

Sometimes the world is crooked. Someone does something so wicked and unnatural everything is bumped from its place and scattered across nature's carpet. Even when the books and knick-knacks are rearranged, everything hangs slightly out of balance.

That's how it felt.

I opened my eyes and handed the gemstone to Joey.

"I have no idea," I admitted.

Joey shook his head and handed the gemstone to Tanner. "Your turn."

Tanner closed his eyes and stuck out his tongue. I know he's mocking me, because of the intense way he does it.

He handed the gemstone back to Joey and leaned back, "Nausea."

Joey made his signature disappointed expression, "You really are insensitive aren't you?"

Tanner nodded sagely, "Yuppie."

We'd all been sitting cross-legged in a circle, like we were children playing a game of stones, or perhaps frogs. We all scooted back a little to let Ginger into the circle.

"Let me try it," she held out her hand expectantly.

"Maybe you shouldn't," Joey said. I know he's not trying to be condescending, but I also know Ginger. She bristled at the implied insult.

"I've made a full recovery since my death, thank you very much. I can handle a little enchantment."

"It's a dark one," Tanner commented, but he plucked the stone from Joey's hand and passed it to Ginger.

She tightened her fist around the stone, and while she didn't close her eyes like I do, her gaze became unfocused as she searched for the feeling of the enchantment.

"I'd guess change, although it's definitely negative. I'm not sure why anyone would want to be imbued with this when they come back."

She set the stone on the ground and flicks it over to Joey. On instinct, Tanner and I both made little goals with our fingers. Joey looked at both of us, sighed, and flicked the gemstone towards me.

It was on target to go right through my fingers, so I shifted them and he missed by a wide margin, "You're as bad at this as you were five years ago! I'd have thought you'd learn!"

Joey gave me a flat look, "you cheat just like you did five years ago."

I flick the gemstone toward Tanner, and he moves his hands just like I did, except the boat rocks and the gemstone skids across

142

the wood on a new trajectory, passing right between his fingers.

"I'm the best," I make finger goals again.

"So what is the enchantment?" Ginger asked.

We'd realized that the man had the names of each enchantment engraved on the stone. That was majorly beneficial to Joey's interpretations, but the rest of us still had to go off emotional response.

"That one was blank," Joey's voice was distant and quiet, as if he was talking to himself. Probably because he was so focused on Tanner's attempts to get the gemstone past my hands.

"You're kidding right?" Ginger glared across the circle. When Joey didn't respond, Ginger slapped her hand down as Tanner flicked the gemstone, and caught the pebble under her palm.

"No, it was blank."

"Well what do you think it was?" Ginger picked up the stone again, trying to gain further insight.

"I was playing with that!" Tanner tried to take it from her, so she raised her hand to keep it from him.

"Why don't we play with," I reached into my bag and withdrew a jewel, "Loved?"

Tanner shook his head, still scrambling for the unknown one, "Bad idea. We might lose it."

Joey tipped a few gems from my bag onto the floor of the cargo hold.

"Why don't you try another unidentified one?" Joey suggested, reaching to pick up one of the stones. Before he could, the boat jostled violently and the amethysts were sent clattering across the space. They scattered behind the boxes and flew into bags and generally made a nuisance of themselves.

"Really Joey?" I snatched my bag from his hands and started picking up all the stones.

"This is a canal! There should not be this many bumps!"

He started shuffling through the bags and boxes beside me. Tanner ditched Ginger and her stone to help find them too.

We didn't worry about noise, we'd been lucky enough to steal onto a boat run by an old deaf man. He had a distinctly withered look, more than just old person rumpledness. I supposed he must've pulled the boats for years, until he'd made just enough to buy his own crew and his own boat. Now he lived out his years in all his grumpy glory, sitting on the deck in his old battered chair.

Tanner smashed one of the boxes to pieces when he accidentally whacked a box with his strength ring.

"You really need to learn to use that thing," I said, shaking sawdust and splinters out of my hair.

"You don't want me to learn how to use it." Tanner said, pocketing a purple gem.

"If you're trying to use reverse psychology it's not working. Also, I saw you take that jewel, and if you don't return it I will throw you off this boat myself."

Tanner ignored the second half of my comment, "You don't want me to use this ring well, because I'll be entirely unstoppable if I do."

"Sure, just try not to knock anyone into next week when you

empty their pockets."

Tanner had started to rummage through the box he'd broken open, and he was grinning like a maniac. From that I could deduct one of two things, he'd found some sharp pointy object he could play with, or he'd found a box full of monkeys. He had a strange fascination with them. Maybe because they shared the same basic personality.

"What did you find Tanner?"

I think the pure dread in my voice made him even more pleased with the discovery. As means of explanation he raised a feathery fabric from the box.

"Today we assume the garb of warriors," he said, throwing the hideous cape over his shoulders.

"That's not ours," Joey said.

"Speak for yourself," Tanner mumbled, continuing to dig through the box.

"Hate to burst your bubble," I walked over to peer into the box, "but I don't think this is warrior stuff. Looks more like the traveling theater."

Tanner gave me a look, "Please. Do you see this?" He raised a bejeweled kilt from the box, "This is what warriors wear."

"And it looks about your size too," I reached into the box and plucked out a red cloak.

I threw it on, and loved the way it swished through the air. When I stood, as regally and puffed up as I could, I imagined it would give a certain elegance to my silhouette.

Tanner, for once, couldn't find anything to laugh at. He did try to offer me an equally red scepter, but I turned it down.

Ginger found herself a nice coat with fur cuffs and a fur collar. Joey told her to put it back, because he could get her a nearly identical one and then it wouldn't be stealing. Tanner pointed out that Joey would probably be getting the jacket from his mother's endless closet, so it actually would be stealing. Ginger kept the jacket.

When we'd gone through the bin twice over and lost interest, we sat on the floor again and tried to identify a few more of the gemstones.

We found direction (which Tanner suggested was to aid in navigation and Joey said was to give the spirit purpose), comforting (which Tanner misidentified as motherly), and lively (which only Ginger guessed correctly).

When that was over we laid against bags of grain and used the costumes as blankets. Thus passed the next few days on the canal. Tanner periodically snuck onto the deck to memorize landmarks and recite them to Joey, who would tell us about how much longer we had on the boat.

Getting off, remarkably, was as easy as getting on. We'd arrived outside the capital late, so the haulers staggered off to get drunk. The owner was asleep on his deck.

We couldn't jump directly onto shore, so we hopped into the shallow water. All except Tanner. His face was ghostly pale in the moonlight, and he shook his head as we tried to coax him into the water.

When he finally did leave the boat, it was by pushing as hard as he could off the rail with his strengthened hand. He launched out over the channel and landed on the muddy shore. Where he promptly slipped into the water.

He flailed about, but before we reached him, he'd pulled himself onto sturdy ground and shook the water out of his ears.

I couldn't help but feel guilty as we trekked toward the front gate. True I hadn't gotten him killed that first time, but I had been the one to give him that fear, in a roundabout way. If it weren't for me he'd be no more afraid of water than he was afraid of the air.

I knew it was illogical–without me he wouldn't even be alive–but it still hurt.

The gate guards let us pass, despite our eclectic clothing, because they'd been given express orders to let in a scraggly bunch of teenagers, described as following: a blonde girl with a suspiciously clinky backpack, a tall professorial teenage boy who looks disappointed in you, a boy with brown hair and a sword that's too big for him, and a black haired girl.

I was slightly miffed at the minimal description I'd gotten, until Joey explained that the head of capital security had met Tanner, Joey, and Ginger separately as part of their conditioning. Once I'd heard that I was extremely happy my description was bland. I would not suffer through long distance training to have a few more words added to my epithet.

The guards told us to go straight to the palace, and told us to follow the main road to avoid unsavory characters. Naturally, since all of us–except Joey–were generally lumped in with unsavory characters, we decided to ignore their advice and go the quickest route.

A 'crippled' beggar healed from their injuries long enough to chase us away from a scattering of coins, but other than that the walk was uneventful.

There was a spot of trouble at the palace gates, as they apparently hadn't been warned of our arrival in the same forthright tones as the gate guards. They'd been told to expect a band of heroes, two girls and two boys, but based on the whole heroes thing they'd assumed we'd be older.

When we were let in, a group of guards escorted us briskly through the corridors. Marie led the group, and when I got a chance, I snuck to the front to talk to her.

"Are we going to be speaking with Kingsman?" I asked.

"Not tonight. We've had guest bedrooms made up for you."

I nodded and sank back to tell the others the good news.

Joey was excited, in his way, and started sharing everything he knew about the King's guest chambers. Apparently the guest wing was first added onto the main palace to house a giant steam engine that would power the entire building. There were structural concerns, and the engineers original plans fell through, so the steam project was abandoned. Instead the wing was converted into a series of guest rooms. The ones in the main wing of the palace were much more decadent, fit for foreign dignitaries and nobles. These were for middle class visitors, essentially. Merchants who could offer important deals to the kingdom, or wealthy artisans who wanted to teach castle staff important skills.

They didn't want to soil four rooms, so Ginger and I shared

one, and Tanner and Joey got another. The rooms were identical. One large bed with rich purple covers, and enough pillows to get lost in. The bare ground had been covered by thick carpets and elegant couches leaned against the walls. Intricate paintings were framed in gold. The overall effect was whelming. The elegance of the room was undermined by the concrete walls peeking out from behind the tapestries. The slightly worn look of the furniture decreased its splendor.

It was sure to be more comfortable and expensive-feeling than anywhere I'd stayed. Anywhere except the noble holiday home I broke into once. I hadn't meant to fall asleep, but I would do it again. Best sleep of my life.

Ginger's fingers traced the carvings on the painting frames, and grazed over the strokes. Her particular attention was focused on a scene, where a maiden in fancy clothing leaned out her tower window to catch a messenger dove on her finger.

"This art is incredible. Do you see the detail on that face?"

I left my bag beside the door, "I like the colors."

Ginger nodded, "That is what love looks like."

"Red and blue?"

"All of it. She's so eager to get the letter. It has to be from her lover. I'll bet he's asking her to run away with him."

Ginger had always been a romantic.

"Why is that love?"

"She's wealthy, obviously. If they ran away, she'd be turning her back on everyone just for them."

"But you said this painting is love. The running away hasn't happened yet," I argued.

Ginger was in a mood for debate, "Fine then. This painting is love because she's so eager to get that letter. No matter what it says, she hopes it's from her special someone."

Tanner chose that exact moment to lean around the doorframe, "whose special someone? I thought you broke up with that merchant Gingy."

"My name is Ginger," she said, walking over to close the door in his face.

"Wait! Do you know when they'll send food?"

Ginger looked over her shoulder at me.

I shrugged, "I don't know if they will. The kitchen staff is probably overworked as it is."

"Goodnight Tanny," Ginger shut the door.

The next morning Kingsman brought us all into his chambers for a briefing. The servants took our weapons, but otherwise left our packs intact. Ginger was forbidden from bringing her potions, and they put cinch bags around Tanner's wrists to discourage him from stealing from the palace. Even with his fingers bound together, I was sure he'd find a way.

Joey and I weren't restricted at all.

"You'll like this guy," I told Joey as we walked up the fifteenth set of stairs, "he's almost as studious as you are."

"He's better informed than I could be. I've read his work, it's the most modern philosophy in our library."

"I didn't know he was a philosopher. I thought his academic interest was mostly political."

"It is. He's a political philosopher. It'll be fascinating to speak to him."

"He's a little odd. He let Tanner die so he could record the results." I didn't add that I'd let him, without so much as arguing. I didn't know Tanner would remember it, but still.

"It seems a little immoral maybe, but the analysis is objectively valuable."

I gave Joey a look.

"I would never do it, but it fits with his philosophy."

When we reached the top of the stairs I realized I wasn't even out of breath. Weeks of walking had gotten me into pretty good shape.

Marie appeared and after an initial pause while she noted our eccentric clothing, she led us toward Kingsman's chambers. She glanced back occasionally, not trying to hide that she was watching Tanner.

When I mentioned this to Tanner, he grinned, "Don't worry. I've nicked three golden baubles."

"How! From what?" I kept my voice at the same low volume as his to keep from arousing suspicion, but Marie turned around and I sidled away from Tanner.

When we reached Kingsman's chambers I was amazed.

The papers that had dominated the space of his desk had multiplied. They were stacked on the floor, old mugs leaving rings on the top. He had a withered houseplant in the corner of his room.

"Welcome back Kennedy, Tanner," he looked at each of us in turn—his eyes taking in my red cloak and Tanner's feather cape with apparent disapproval–, "and welcome Joey and Ginger."

"Pleased to meet you," Joey said, bowing slightly.

Ginger took the cue and bowed too, so I did as well. Tanner either didn't notice or didn't care.

"I got an alarming report from Billingsley. He said the Piper had joined forces with Daemon John."

"Yes sir. Daemon John arrived at the Inn with a group of the Piper's known associates," Joey explained concisely.

"And John wasn't possessed? He seemed in control of his faculties?"

Joey nodded, but before he could speak, Tanner jumped in.

"Yes the journey was troublesome but we made it out alive. The Piper is still free, Daemon John has ulterior motives, and the King used children to protect himself. Now to the real problem. Are we pardoned for our crimes?"

Kingsman leaned forward, "He used you to protect himself? Is that really how you feel?"

This time I spoke over Joey, "Of course not, Kingsman. Tanner is just saying that because that's how Daemon framed it."

Kingsman leaned back in his chair, picked up one of his dozen mugs and seemed content to just hold it.

"Oh, and please answer Tanner's question. I'm actually curious." I said.

Kingsman cleared his throat, "Your mission was to take down the Piper. You didn't do that."

A chorus of inhaled breaths and the beginnings of arguments later and George Kingsman raised a hand to quiet us.

"You did risk your lives–"

"We didn't just risk them!" Tanner corrected, "We all died!"

"Except for Kennedy," Joey added.

"Are you going to withhold payment from Joey and I because we didn't catch the piper?" Ginger asked.

That took me aback. I supposed it was only right that they were going to be paid somehow for escorting me and Tanner, but I'd never truly considered it. I aimlessly wondered how much they had cost.

"You were simply hired to accompany the criminals and assist them. There is no reason you should not be paid in full."

Tanner balked, and tried to make a statement several times before he shrank back in defeat.

"You will receive a partial pardon, for the injuries you sustained, par the course of the mission. You will not, however, be freed entirely. The contract was that you would be released only upon the capture of the Piper or the disbanding of the army."

I only hazily remembered the contract. They'd shoved a paper under my nose before we left, covered in elegant calligraphy I had no capability to read. Seemed a little low to make an illiterate person sign a binding contract. I hadn't even been able to write my name. I'd just scrawled a weird little scribble at the bottom.

"That contract was a sham. Neither of us can read," I said.

Kingsman shrugged, and the impression I had of him slipped away like oil. Somehow, despite his occupation and status, I'd forgotten he was a general. He seemed more like a student, obsessed with his notes and everything he could learn. No student would get to the position he was in though, simply by thought experiments. I remembered what Joey had said on our way to his chambers. Kingsman had let Tanner die, simply so he could record notes.

Why would he care that it was an unfair contract? He could've assumed we'd fail, and I'm sure he did. Why else would he phrase the contract in such a way?

This should've discouraged me, the immorality, the unfairness, but it felt like a revelation. No, not a revelation, an epiphany. I understood Kingsman better. His motives were study, and advancement. His political philosophy was essentially anything for the greater good, the ends justify the means and all that. Perhaps he had some unique twists, but that seemed to be the basis.

Kingman tugged a thin cord near the wall, and Marie appeared almost instantly. Kingsman asked her to escort Ginger and Joey from the palace and give them their payments. They protested, but the bustling efficiency of Marie quickly overwhelmed them.

She also found time to clear the chairs in front of Kingsman's desk of their papers, and Tanner and I sat down. Tanner tipped, almost immediately, onto the two back legs. I was struck by deja vu.

"I suggest a new deal. It'll expedite your release from servitude," Kingsman proposed.

Tanner nodded eagerly, but I had a feeling I knew what was coming.

"A study of death. We will experiment with new toxins, poisons, and traps for a few weeks. Tanner, you would have to die several times over, but Kennedy will be there to revive you."

Tanner's face paled visibly, and he swallowed hard, "How many weeks would this testing last?"

"Given the partial pardon, you have seven years left of your sentence, if you don't take this offer."

It was much better than a life sentence, but seven years felt like a lifetime.

"The testing would last three to twelve months, and then you'd be freed."

Tanner leaned forward and the front two legs thumped down on the floor, "We'll need an exact number for the length of testing, and we need Joey to read the contracts this time, but other than that we'll do it."

Just like last time, Tanner was speaking for the both of us. Except this time, I spoke up.

"No. We won't be doing that." Tanner immediately began to protest, but I spoke over him.

"We have information that wasn't disclosed to your agent, Billingswhatever. We can share it with you."

Kingsman's face remained composed, but I'd gotten a glimpse of his psyche. I knew what he was mulling over.

"And don't even think that torture could get you the same answers. We both know that after literally dying and everything else we've been through, your torture wouldn't work. Furthermore," I was proud of myself for using that word, a word

I'd only ever heard Joey use, "it could be essential to stopping the Piper and Daemon John before their army really starts a war."

The Kingsman finally took a sip out of his mug, he winced as he leaned forward to set it down.

"I also have a cure for your back pain," that was an educated guess. He'd winced in a similar way before, and the way he moved, which before had just seemed strange, now seemed to be a result of injuries.

"You realize it's treasonous to keep information from the General regarding war matters?" he leveled his plain eyes at me.

"Then hang us," Tanner winked at me and he looked remarkably more like himself when he tipped back onto two legs.

Kingman clenched his jaw, and I felt a pang of exultation. He had probably made enemies on his way up the social ladder, but this was likely the first time they were teenagers.

Kingsman sighed, "I suppose you make fair points. Before we begin the discussion, how did you discover my back pain?"

I bit my cheeks to keep from grinning, "The way you move."

"And the cure?"

"Isn't it obvious? One quick slice of the neck, one quick revival, and your entire body is rebuilt as new."

He looked down, but not before I caught the glitter of interest in his eyes. He was fascinated by the idea of personal experience with death, and the revival process. He was no fool, so of course he was suspicious that I wouldn't bring him back.

He proved his suspicions when he said, "If you left me dead you wouldn't be freed. Your contract would remain, and you'd be

156

forced to serve out your seven years. Almost no one even knows about the Piper, and many fewer know about your involvement. My successor would have no reason to make deals with you."

"I know. I will revive you."

Kingsman still hesitated.

"I'd say that is worth a year of servitude, on its own. You're healed of a lasting injury, and you get firsthand knowledge of necromancy that can be recorded in your journals. As for the information, since it could stop the death of hundreds of citizens and a possible war, I'd say that knocks off the rest."

Kingsman reached for a pen, and started to scribble something onto a blank sheet of paper, "I accept your terms for the necromancy..." he said. I almost didn't catch the words, I was so focused on the way his pen moved so fast it blurred in the air.

"But not for the information. Because you're engaging in treasonous behavior, I cannot reward you with a full six years. It is worth something though, so I promise you'll be paid wages–although slight–and you'll be permitted to return home in the evenings."

"That's unacceptable," I said, at the same time Tanner said, "That sounds like a real job."

Kingsman's hand slowed, and the pen left a blot on the page.

"You are not in a place to be bargaining here," Kingsman said, and when he looked up, his simple face seemed wrought with fervor in every line.

I didn't allow it to scare me, "I don't know. The most I can lose is a few years. You're trying to bargain a kingdom. I think I'm doing just fine."

Tanner laughed.

Kingsman gritted his teeth again, "I suppose so. Still, it's hard to make a deal for information without knowing what it'll be. Perhaps we can draw up an agreement–"

"Not without Joey here," Tanner stated.

Negotiations continued in a similar vein for about ten minutes. I tried to replicate the way Ginger and Joey argued, picking out grammatical meanings, and overanalyzing word choice. Tanner confronted Kingsman's opinions boldly and without hesitation. Together we wore down Kingsman until he agreed to the following: we would provide him with our information, and whether he liked it or not, instead of seven years of servitude, we would be sent on another mission. If the information was bad, we'd have very little choice in what the mission was or who to do it with (he made it very clear the mission would involve studying and researching death). If the information was good however, we could pick between several different options for missions, choose who to work with, and most of the terms.

Once the information was shared, and the details figured out, George Kingsman would take one of many poisons he knew were stored in the palace, for everything from killing vermin to torturing the prisoners. I'd revive him, and instead of it knocking a year off our sentence, our families would be paid for essentially lending us out.

It would be a very small sum, but Tanner and I definitely ended up ahead in the whole exchange. At least, that's what I'd

158

assumed.

Kingsman found a blank sheet of paper, and readied his pen in one hand and a mug in the other.

"So what is this incredibly important information?"

"Daemon John is planning another revolution," I said, with all the drama I could muster.

After a few seconds, Kingsman looked up from his blank page, "You're kidding right? That's not all there is?"

I shook my head, "No, that's not all, but that's the key idea."

Kingsman set his mug on the corner of the desk, "We already knew he was working with the Piper on his army."

"True, but that's not what I'm talking about," Tanner was listening to my words as avidly as Kingsman, "I'm talking about a real rebellion. Sure he has his possessed zombie army, but he's been working on something else for far longer."

Kingsman wrote something on the paper, but his pen moved slowly, moving with much more deliberation than before. I imagined that maybe he was writing out the official way the death study would be carried out. I swallowed that fear down and continued.

"Ever heard of Befreiung der Verdammten?"

Tanner wobbled on the legs of his chair and flailed his arms to keep from tipping back. Kingsman looked up at me, his pen having just made a jagged line across the page.

"We don't have physical evidence that proves he's the leader, but signs point to him. First, he was wearing purple, the infamous color of the cult, because they want to associate with royalty.

Second, all of the men at the Inn were members, and kept talking about endings."

Before I could finish my list, which was rather small, Kingsman cut in, "Are you suggesting die Befreiten–"

"Don't call them that. It acknowledges that they really are liberated, and they aren't," I stated.

Kingsman nodded with the air of trying to get back to his thoughts, "You're suggesting Daemon John is behind the Befreiung der Verdammten theology, all for the purpose of overthrowing the King?"

I nodded, "Yes. Daemon John is famous for his traps. I was attacked when I was in the prison, so obviously the cult has people everywhere. If they really wanted to overthrow the king, the perfect trap is in motion. They have an army to scare the populous into behaving. Not to mention they have actual followers stationed in the palace and across every kingdom of the known world to act as assassins or in whatever capacity the cult leader suggests!"

Kingsman had written down most of what I'd said, or at least I assumed that's what he was writing.

"For an uneducated youth, you seem very confident in your answers."

I felt anger boil in my stomach, but I knew insulting him back wouldn't be the best path forward, no matter how much I wanted it to be.

Instead I kept my voice calm, "I am confident because I know what I'm talking about. My education has nothing to do with it."

160

Kingsman cleared his throat, "Perhaps it doesn't, but if you were properly educated you'd know that the focus of Befreiung der Verdammten is resurrection. There are no aspects of the theology that lend themselves to religious war or attacks."

"Be that as it may," an edge had crept into my voice at his dismissal of our discoveries, "the members follow their leader with absolute devotion. If you don't trust me, ask Joey. His family is known for their extensive library, and he's known even in noble circles as a prodigy. He loved talking about how the cultists faith is bought, because the gemstones they believe will revive them are only supplied by the leader. If the leader threatens to withhold them they'd do anything, but it probably wouldn't even come to that. Their gratitude goes beyond reason, and they do not fear death because they believe they'll come back," I was talking fast, as if to get in all the words before Kingsman's eyes glazed over again, "It's actually perfect as a revolutionary system, the youngest and most fearless would be willing to take great risks to earn more expensive gemstones they couldn't otherwise afford. The King is in danger, and if Daemon becomes king, everyone in this kingdom is in danger."

I only stopped ranting because I needed to breathe.

For some unknown reason Kingsman was smiling faintly, "Good arguments, Kennedy. I'm impressed."

"I'm not done," I said, suddenly frantic with worry it hadn't been enough, "the men around Daemon John all accepted him as their leader, and they were adorned with any number of rare gemstones. Part of their belief is that they should rarely submit to authority, except that of their spiritual leaders, so for such high up members to submit to anyone but a King or noble, it would be essentially a betrayal of their religion. Daemon John is clearly the leader."

"I still think I could have caught him if I wasn't so busy saving you all," Tanner said.

"Yes you were very heroic," I accepted, "I just have one more thing to say. The piper didn't take the risk of meeting with us, which shows that he's much more cautious. I'd assume he's not a member of the cult, which means he may not understand everything that's going on with Befreiung der Verdammten."

Kingsman had added several more words to the paper, the letters becoming more cramped as he ran out of space. When he finally replaced his pen with his mug, and sat back in his chair, his eyebrows were drawn in a way that suggested serious reflection.

"If you did extra service for the crown, after your mission of course, I may be able to enroll you in a school."

The anger I'd felt at his condescension immediately evaporated, and the steam of it made me feel dizzy.

Kingsman set down his cup, "that is good information. Even without proof, it cannot be dismissed without serious considerations. I will have my agents look into this. In the meantime, I have a new mission."

"Only one? George, our information was definitely as good as we promised, we should be given options!" Tanner's main consideration most of the time was how he could become famous, so it struck me as out of character that he'd ask for options, because the obvious assumption was that we'd pick the easiest. I understood when he turned to face me, his expression said it all. He was trying to tell me my arguments had been good.

Kingsman reassured us, "There will be plenty of options, and plenty of time to debate the terms of our argument. No matter what though, there is someone you should meet."

Chapter 13
The Piper

My eyes opened, and for a moment the whole world seemed a blur of black and brown. Then my vision cleared, bars sprung from the shadows, and various shades of brown assembled themselves into ragged clothing and three people.

"Kennedy, Tanner, I introduce the Pied Piper," the tallest of the three said.

He had the face of a laborer, the demeanor of a noble, and the deportment of a soldier. Thin lines were carved at the edges of his mouth and the corners of his eyes. They didn't make him look particularly old, rather lending a look like the youth had been sapped out of him.

The second tallest, a brown haired boy, looked like so many others from the orphanage. He wore a cape of black feathers though, one I'd only ever seen shamans dawn. He didn't carry himself like a magick man, his fingers rolled a ring between them, a habit of pickpockets. His gaze wasn't darting, but something about the way he stared gave the impression he saw everything. It wouldn't have surprised me at all if he was being introduced as my cellmate.

The third was a girl. She had the lean muscle of the village engineers, and her eyes had the same shrewd intelligence. A red cloak hung from her soldiers, giving her a regal appearance, although the calluses on her hands and the scars on her arms marked her as a street kid, and not a noble. Her features weren't harsh, but her expression emphasized them in a way that made me feel analyzed.

The last two stood a little apart from the man, and closer together than two casual acquaintances.

The cobbled floor had the same texture as the street on the night of the Summer Festival, but the smell of the dungeon was much more similar to the battleground of the red rebellion.

I stood up slowly, and I'll have you know, I did a remarkable job of keeping my expression neutral.

My first attempts to remember where I was, or how I'd gotten there, were unsuccessful, especially when the boy, Tanner I assumed, interrupted.

"You never said he was a kid," he was clearly addressing the adult, but he was staring at me.

I narrowed my eyes at him. My initial impression was of another street savvy boy, but I understood he was fundamentally different that I had been. Most of the street kids I knew were the kind who'd been humbled by life. They had no qualms with begging for food, or pretending weakness to gain an advantage.

This boy had been hardened in his pride, becoming reckless instead of spiritless.

I too addressed the adult when I spoke, "where am I?"

My voice was raspy from disuse.

The man smiled pleasantly, although absently, "You are in the palace dungeons."

I cannot express properly the way the light seemed to flare in that moment. Maybe it was simply the intensity of the situation. Regardless, I hunched away from the light, as if the darkness would embrace me and hide me somewhere safer.

"Did Daemon John really turn you in to the army?"

This time it was the girl who spoke. The words shocked the world back into its regular dimness, and I reigned in my breathing.

I tried to remember. My throat itched, a reminder of the snake's constriction.

"Yes," I tried to discreetly check my pockets for my pipe.

"They took your whistle buddy," Tanner said, "it would be no use anyway. We aren't adults, if you couldn't tell," he gestured at himself and the girl.

The man waved at someone out of sight down the hall, and soon a few guards were on their way over. They unlocked my cell, and bound thick manacles around my hands and chains to my feet. Years of instinct kicked my heart into high gear, and my vision narrowed. I nearly made a break for it, but I thought better of it. Despite myself I was curious.

I want to make sure you understand, so I'll explain. In that dim dungeon, so like many places I'd hidden, I was buried in so many sensations. Remembrances of the past layered over the present until everything was disorienting. Whatever drug had kept me asleep was still hanging heavy on my brain, and impeding my usual thought. What's more, there was a strange familiarity about the teenagers. Not their physical features, although I recognized those, no it was in their attitudes. The way their faces were set, the unique mix of immaturity and emotional depth that made up heroes, it made them instantly similar to every hero I'd dreamt of as a kid. With all these thoughts at work, is it any wonder curiosity won the day?

I looked at the girl as the guards led me from the cell, "are you the necromancer?"

The guards shook me roughly, and one prodded me and told me to stop talking nonsense.

Still, I saw the girl nod, just slightly, before we started down the hall.

The man who'd been with them in the beginning gave a few orders to the guards then retreated down the hall. The girl and boy followed behind, their footsteps barely audible over the clinking of my chains.

I'd forgotten what it was like to just walk. Not whistling, not commanding an army at my back, not attempting to keep a snake at arms length. Strange as it seems, walking through that dungeon was one of the most leisurely strolls I ever took.

It took several minutes before we reached other occupied cells, and when the sounds of people struck me, I stopped without meaning to. A sob escaped my throat before I realized it was trapped there.

I hadn't heard so many in such a long time. It wasn't loud, but the quiet was filled with all the small shufflings of life. A small number of prisoners were humming or consciously making noise, but most of it was just the filling sound of living.

It made me realize how much life had been missing from my travels with the army. Sure Daemon and his followers had been there, but they were so few and far between, they lacked the same quality of humanity.

The children didn't introduce themselves until we'd arrived at a large closed off cell. The ceiling hung low, and instead of bars, there were walls. The area was suffocating, and when the chains were attached to the wall, it only enhanced the feeling.

"Hello, I'm Kennedy," the girl said.

"You can call her Edy, and I'm Tanner," the boy stepped forward as if to shake my hand, and when I raised my manacle, he took that instead and shook it vigorously.

When I didn't say anything they looked at each other, and after some kind of silent conversation, the girl stepped forward.

"Is Daemon John connected to Befreiung der Verdammten?"

I shrugged.

It wasn't that I didn't want to speak, quite the opposite in fact, but I didn't know how to address heroes.

After another silent communication between the two of them, the girl turned to me again.

"Are you part of his rebellion? Is that why you made the army?"

I knew the answer to that one, "No."

After another pause, the girl's hesitant manor dropped away, like she'd made the decision to be clear.

"We fought your men at the Inn. I'm not sure if you knew this or not, but they were all members of Befreiung der Verdammten. We believe Daemon wants to use the cult and your army to overthrow the King."

"I wanted to be King." I said. I bowed my head, because looking at the floor was easier than looking at their faces. The stones beneath my feet were worn smooth by previous prisoners, who'd also left scarlet stains between the stones, like a thin stream.

"Why?" Tanner asked.

I sat as best I could against the wall, and wrapped my arms around my knees. I didn't answer immediately, but they both seemed conscious that I intended to answer eventually so they didn't push me.

"I thought people loved kings. I changed my mind."

I heard the boy draw in a breath to say something, but the girl gave him a look and he didn't speak.

My manacles traced circles on the ground, "People don't love the King. They just have to pretend."

Kennedy shifted her bag on her shoulder until she could reach in. She pulled out a bottle of water, unscrewed it and handed it to me. Her expression hadn't lost its analytical quality, but it had softened.

"Drink up."

It was hard to clutch the bottle between the manacles, but I appreciated that she hadn't tried to pour it down my throat.

I was grateful for the gesture itself just as much or more. She gave me her own water. True she could be bribing me for knowledge, but she had to know I didn't know much. Which meant she'd done it because she saw my need.

I gulped down half the bottle before I set it awkwardly on the ground and wiped my chin on my shoulder.

"Daemon probably took my army. I told them to obey him like they obeyed me." That wasn't what I wanted to say. I wanted to say that I wanted to be a hero. I wanted to say I could join them. It wasn't that I couldn't find the words–there are so many words it's almost impossible not to find them–it was that I couldn't get them past the fear in my throat.

"So he acted as your general then?" Kennedy asked.

I nodded, and tightened my arms around my knees, "I knew he would betray me. He's a snake."

Kennedy nodded, and bit her lip, "Do you still want him to have your army? To overthrow the King?"

I shook my head, and stared at her boots. They were quality boots, probably provided by the palace, there's no other way the sole would be so thick. The leather too was high quality, although it was scuffed from use.

"How old are you?" Tanner asked, sitting down on the floor to look across the chambers at me. He ran a hand through his hair, and I caught a glimpse of silver on his finger.

Age was a sensitive topic. They weren't sure how old I was when I'd been dropped at the orphanage. I wasn't a newborn at least, which was rare. Since then, I'd grown taller, and lived through many winters, but they'd never celebrated any birthdays. I knew they kept track of seasons to know when to kick me out, but they never told us what they knew.

I shrugged, "Don't know."

Kennedy's expression was still firm with determination, but the quality of her eyes changed, and I knew she was beginning to pity me.

Pity had been a good thing, sometimes it meant a few coins tossed our way, or an extra blanket when we were sick. This time I knew it wasn't good, because the pity crawled like termites across my skin, burrowing into me and making we weak.

If I was going to be a hero, I could not be weak.

"Daemon said there were four of you at the Inn. Where is the witch and the other swordsman?"

Tanner puffed out his cheeks as he breathed out, "since they're not criminals, they're back to their lives,"

That confirmed my suspicions. Tanner must be a thief, what had Kennedy done? She move like a pick-pocket, but I suppose I couldn't be sure.

That also disappointed me slightly. A band of heroes should always be together, shouldn't they? I quickly reconciled the idea, heroes had lives outside their work. They had to.

"You said Daemon wanted to overthrow the King," I spoke quietly, afraid that if I spoke loudly the words would break their friendliness.

Kennedy nodded, and looked as if she wanted to say

something, but I had to get the words out.

"I want to help you stop him. I want to be a hero."

Tanner grinned, and Kennedy's eyes narrowed in thought.

"Well then!" Tanner exclaimed, "you'd be pretty helpful if you wanted to be."

Kennedy was more suspicious, but she was too tactful to say she distrusted me to my face, instead she settled for saying, "We might not be sent to stop him, now that you're not working with them."

"Heroes go on all kinds of missions. It doesn't matter if you're not old, or if someone else could do it." I said.

"I like this kid," Tanner said, "We are heroes aren't we Edy?"

Kennedy let out a breath like a laugh, "Of course Tanner. Have all your wildest dreams come true?"

"Not yet. We've made it to heroes, but that's still a far cry from legends."

"Stopping an army would get you there," I said, quietly, pensively.

Kennedy sighed, "We can't stop an army though, we were hired just to find you."

Tanner looked excited, "Wait Edy we could do it! We can pick that as our mission, and we could pick the piper as one of the members!"

"We don't know enough! Daemon could be giving any kind of orders! Besides, a normal army could fight him off now."

"But what about Befreiung der Verdammmten? No one really

knows what they're doing?" Tanner stood up, and started to pace off the energy.

I looked back at the rivulets of red that had been left in the seams between stones. Kennedy and Tanner kept talking, but I lost focus, and it turned to a background hum. What would happen if Daemon actually attacked the palace?

He'd have me put to death. Was that what the current king was going to do? I traced a trail of blood with my eyes. I was a threat, I knew that.

I think it was the absolute certainty that I was going to die if I didn't get out of there that drove me to action. I stood up, and the jangling of my chains immediately put an end to their argument.

"Hundreds of people will die if Daemon's army and the King's armies fight. Why don't we go to the battlefield and stop them? If I had my pipe I could stop the armies from fighting at all."

Tanner gestured aggressively at me, "Exactly!"

"Please Edy. If I can't do this I think they'll hang me."

The sudden stillness in the air told me they believed the same. Kennedy shook her head, as if she was trying to get water from her ears.

"It's not up to us. Kingsman will decide your fate."

Tanner rolled his eyes, "We can bring it up though, persuade him."

"Thank you. Thank you both."

Kennedy opened her mouth as if to say something, then turned and stepped from the cell.

Tanner winked at me, "You're welcome. And don't worry, I'll convince George to give it a try."

Chapter 14
Kennedy

As soon as we were out of the guard's earshot I rounded on Tanner.

"Tanner, that boy is a piper! He enchanted several towns for goodness sake! We can't just invite him to join us!"

"He may be a piper, but he's just a kid. He's not evil or anything, and besides, it's not a bad idea. We can't stop the army, but maybe he could." I knew Tanner's argument was based on more than just logic, the kid had an uncanny resemblance to one of Tanner's younger brothers.

"I feel bad for the kid too, but it's not like we can just invite him along! What if he blindsides us? What if he sics the army on us?"

"We could just knock him out or something. C'mon Edy, it would be legendary."

That it would be. The problem is most legends die young. Tanner was living proof, in a way.

"I told you to stop calling me Edy."

Marie caught up with us after that, and put our discussion to an end.

As we ascended the steps, I thought it over in my head. The boy had certainly looked harmless enough, but I couldn't just dismiss what he'd done. Besides, it wasn't like there weren't other ways to end this. There had to be some other way, a way where I wouldn't have to rely on a stranger. Although I supposed that's what the King had done when he sent us, relied on young strangers to save the Kingdom, because no one else could.

My thoughts were stalled when we were shuffled into the Kingsman's chambers. The discussion with him went about how I'd expected it to. There was a lot of talking and debating, and a lot of staring into the distance like it had all the answers. Tanner did most of the talking, and I knew he'd picked up some tricks from Ginger and Joey on our trip, because a few of his points really threw Kingsman into a loop.

In the end, Kingsman agreed to speak to the King about an offensive with the piper. He said that in the meantime, his back was hurting and it was about time I healed it.

He laid down on the floor, so it would be easy for me to arrange him, he said. Then he handed Tanner a vial of the most potent poison he had on hand. He had both of us cover our mouths and noses with cloth so we couldn't breathe it in.

Kingsman opened his mouth, and Tanner let a single drop fall from the vial. Kingsman closed his mouth, but not before a whisper of smoke escaped. The life left his open eyes a second later, and trails of steam wound up from his nostrils.

Tanner corked the vial and tucked it into some hidden pocket or another. We both stepped back just in case, until the steam dissipated.

Then I checked nothing was wrong with the way he'd laid down. I didn't spot any errors, so I reached out to bring him back.

Something was wrong. Very very wrong. His skin flecked away like rust, and new epidermis replaced it, rippling and stretching over his bones and muscles. The process looked the way it always did, but it felt wrong.

I'd never felt it before. I'd never felt energy draining away from me as the person came back, but this time I did. I stumbled back from his body, even as it stilled and returned to life.

"Woah!" Tanner shouted, and he stepped over Kingsman to catch me as I toppled over.

"Are you ok Kennedy?"

He was spinning, or was I?

"I'm fine, just let me sit."

Tanner held onto my arm until I was sitting against the wall. I would've hated the concern in his face, if I'd been able to focus on it.

As it was, I couldn't focus on anything. It all seemed to be undulating closer and further away, and spinning. Everything was spinning.

In the middle of the room Kingsman was breathing steadily. He sat up, and looked at his hands as if he'd never seen them before.

"Kennedy, did you breathe in the steam? Was it the poison?"

I shook my head, "No, I'm fine."

Except I wasn't and we both knew it. I blinked, and almost couldn't open my eyes, and that should've scared me except I couldn't feel anything but a vague heat.

"Kennedy? Edy? What's going on, what are you feeling?"

The words sounded like they were coming through water, echoing and hitting my eardrums with a strange pressure.

Kingsman stood up, and put a hand on Tanner's shoulder, "She won't die, trust me."

Tanner turned on him, "Did you do this? What did you do?"

He shoved Kingsman with both hands, and Kingsman fell backwards, falling against his desk.

"Calm down Tanner," He said, pushing himself cautiously off the desk, "she'll be fine in just a second."

"What did you do?" Tanner stood just in front of Kingsman, his fist raised threateningly.

The world was settling down, my focus returning.

"I said I was fine," I pushed against the wall and tried to stand but my arms were too weak and I fell back.

"You are not fine," Tanner said, but he left Kingsman to come kneel by me.

"What happened?" He asked.

I looked at Kingsman, and he took my cue and answered the question.

"You just healed me from a curse lasting over twelve years," he said.

Tanner and I both gaped.

"You see, I was cursed with stagnation. The small cuts and injuries I had never healed, my back, which had just been tweaked and should've healed normally, remained in the same state of sensitivity. Besides death, my physiological state could not change."

"I think you mean physical state," Tanner corrects.

Kingsman shakes his head, "No I mean physiological…or I suppose not. I could change emotions, but I could not grow. I haven't written philosophy in years because I was not able to come up with anything new."

"Is that why bringing you back was so hard? You were cursed not to change?" My voice was surprisingly weak.

"I believe so."

"Can we get water or something?" Tanner asked, glaring up at Kingsman, then he looked back at me, "You sound like you could use some water."

"Yes I'll send for," Kingsman stopped halfway through the sentence and halfway to the chord that would call Marie.

"Actually," he said, a smile growing on his face, "I'll go get it. I can walk more now, it doesn't hurt nearly as bad. Yes, a trip down the stairs would be good."

Kingsman wanted us to come with him at first, but relented when I could barely even stand up. Instead he moved us to a room next to his office, which was originally designed to be a kind of waiting room.

There was a table in the center of the room, and sofas lined the walls. There were no elegant rugs in this room, but the hard wood floors were just as majestic.

I tried to walk on my own, but I kept knocking into walls and nearly falling on my face, so I grudgingly let Tanner act as my crutch.

He helped me to one of the couches and I sat down with relief. I breathed deeply until the world really stopped spinning and my nausea died down.

"Is it normally tiring to revive us?" Tanner was leaning back on a separate couch, his posture the kind of casual only people pretending to be casual adopt.

"Not at all. I've never even felt a change." I swallowed, and felt my pounding heart in my throat. I'd always accepted that I didn't understand my powers, but this changed things. My powers weren't boundless. I'd never really thought they were, but there was a part of me–a small part–that had hoped.

"Are you feeling a little better now? Better than you were at first?"

"Yeah, I am."

Kingsman appeared with three glasses in hand, and set them out on the table.

I reached forward to get mine, and my hands were shaking so badly I spilled half of the water before I even got a sip.

Tanner and Kingsman were polite enough to pretend not to notice.

"As per our deal, your families will be receiving wages for every week you spend on the mission."

Tanner shook his head, "I know that's what we agreed to, but that's before we knew you were cursed. It wasn't fair to put Edy through that."

"Back to Edy huh?" I muttered under my breath.

"We had a contract."

"A contract for a normal necromancy, not for that!" Tanner leaned forward as he was struck by an idea, "You can change now. You can change what you think we deserve for the service we provided."

Kingsman laughed, a hearty sound, "that's so juvenile! Did you really think that would persuade me?"

"Edy healed both your back, which was the agreement, and your curse. That was not in the contract so we should receive more compensation."

Kingsman was still chuckling softly when he answered, "fine fine. I'm in a good mood. What do you want?"

Tanner looked across at me, "Up to you Kennedy."

I hesitated, and hoped that my decision wasn't fueled by confusion and the lingering effects of healing a curse. In the end, I came to the decision that my choice was for the greater good, and it would benefit everyone if it succeeded.

"I want us to be legends."

It was that simple. We were sent off to war.

However wrong Daemon John was, he was right about one thing. The King had no qualms with hiding behind children. He agreed almost immediately to send the piper, accompanied by Tanner and I, to disband the approaching army. We'd tried to persuade Kingsman to let Ginger and Joey join us, but he–with sudden morality–said they weren't necessary, and risking their lives or harm wasn't worth it.

We didn't really need his permission.

While our packs were once again being prepared, and all Kingsman's research staff decided what we'd do, Tanner and I were sent to the dungeons to tell the piper the news.

When we began the final descent into the dungeons, the servants left us to tend to other chores. Tanner and I looked at each other and grinned.

We'd paid one of the lesser servants to write out a simple message. Tanner had a few more baubles he'd taken from his stroll through the palace halls, and we would bribe one of the guards to deliver the message for us.

Tanner winked and ducked from the hall for a quiet minute, before he returned, his hands empty of any cryptic messages.

"Time to get the piper then?"

He was in the cell he'd been in when we first arrived, and they'd removed the manacles and chains. They'd left rings of red around his wrists and ankles. Dirt was caked onto his skin, but it didn't hide the vitiligo. He wore clothing that was slightly less dirty than the rest of him, but it didn't fit right. I assumed he'd taken it from some adult or another.

He looked young when he was hunched over, but when he looked up, the maturity in his face reminded me he wasn't a child. He might be about my age, or just a year or so younger.

"We're going to do it," Tanner announced, playing with the

keys the servants had given him. Personally, I wouldn't trust him with any kind of important keys–he was bound to do impulsive things–but it was their funeral.

"Stop the army?" the piper asked. His voice was dry again. He stood up, and tugged on his shirt to adjust the way it hung.

"Yeah. Ready to be a hero?"

Tanner was all smiles. I tried to look excited too, but I had reservations. It would be so easy for the piper to turn on us and take back control of the army.

Part of our mission was to take him out of commission if it looked like he was going to go rogue. If he did, we'd be tasked with returning his body, and reviving him so he could be hanged publicly.

Publicly, because the King had officially announced that the army was marching on the capital. He'd held off, hoping we'd take out the army, or that without the Piper, they'd return on their own to their lives. He made the attack official, to give Kingsman more room to maneuver as well. With an official attack pending, Kingsman had permission to clear people from towns, and draft men and women into the army.

Naturally the kingdom had an army already, but it was small. We had treaties with all the neighboring kingdoms, so keeping a large army was a waste of funds.

While Tanner went to work on the seven locks, I held a hand through the bars to the boy.

"I know we already had introductions, but we forgot to ask your name, so let's try again," the boy took my outstretched hand

and we shook, "I'm Kennedy."

The boy swallowed, "Nice to meet you Kennedy."

I nodded, hoping he'd pick up that I was waiting for his name.

"Daemon never asked my name," he said instead.

"Well we already knew Daemon wasn't a good person," I laughed lightly. It was a fake laugh, to make him more comfortable, but it wasn't unconvincing.

The boy dropped my hand and looked down at his feet. His toes were peeking through an old pair of boots.

"I'm Fitz," he said quietly.

"Well Fitz, I'm delighted to make your acquaintance. I brought you a gift," I pulled a shining flute from an inside pocket of my cloak.

He looked at it in wonder and his fingers twitched as if anticipating the feeling of the instrument in them, "I don't know how to play a flute."

The last lock clicked, and Tanner swung the door open, "Doesn't matter Fitz. Anything you play will work."

A puzzled look flashed across his face until he schooled his expression into casually curious.

"The whistle wasn't magickal?"

I shook my head. Tanner and I had known it would be dangerous to reveal that his magick had nothing to do with the pipe before we got out. We'd decided it would be a good test. He couldn't do much in a dungeon, but if he really planned to betray us and take over, he was likely to make a move.

184

Fitz didn't so much as try to leave his cell before we invited him too.

"We have to head out as fast as possible, so Edy is going to take you outside. I'm going to grab the packs," Tanner explained. In truth, a servant would meet him at the gate. He had to separate to snag a few things from the palace for Ginger and Joey, when they met us.

"So you're from Kartoffelstadt?" I asked Fitz. I was nearly sure that's what Joey had said.

Fitz nodded, "I'm from the orphanage there."

I sucked in a harsh breath. The Kartoffeistadt orphanage was infamous for their immoral treatment of the kids in their care. Unfortunately the funding for such institutions was so low there were never any corrections.

My desire to console him warred with my desire to remain quiet and see what else he'd say. The later desire won out.

We walked in silence for a minute.

"They didn't know my name either. They only ever learned the names of the pretty children."

He spoke with an attitude of determination, like he just wanted to get it all out.

"I named myself. I thought King Fitz would have a good ring to it. I know Fitz is a common last name, but I want to make sure they still call me Fitz when we're all legends."

I almost laughed. He had very similar priorities to Tanner.

"We'll make sure."

Fitz smiled. He had a quiet smile. It wasn't a smile for

anyone else, but its sincerity gave it its own gravity.

"I know they called me the Pied Piper…"

Everytime he heard that name he must've been reminded of the workers at the orphanage, the one's notorious for starving the children who they didn't think would earn them money from adoptions.

"…but I think Flute-y Fitz has a good ring to it too."

"Perfect for the bards. Although, I suppose you could write your own ballads, couldn't you," I paused to see if he'd respond. When he didn't I said, "Tanner used to call himself Light Bringer."

That was before he'd ever died. I remembered him announcing the name from the top of a staircase. He had stood at the top, with his hands on his hips. His fingers glittered with stolen jewelry, and there was a gaudy bangle around his ankle, although he wasn't wearing shoes. The sun had been rising behind him, and with only his silhouette visible I'd thought that maybe he really could bring the light.

"We told stories about heroes sometimes," Fitz's voice was quiet, "I think one of them was called that."

That was news to me, "Really?" I regretted it the minute I said it. It was just a simple question, but it led to a story. The voice he adopted when he spoke was like his smile, simple and quiet, but magnetic. I wanted to lean in to hear what he said, but I couldn't afford that, I may be tasked with the unpleasant duty of killing him.

"The sun fell out of the sky once. The stars tried to replace it, but they just weren't bright enough. There was a boy, the son of a

186

blacksmith, who decided he was going to find it and return it to its place. There are so many different ways we said he found it but the ending was always the same. He leapt from the highest mountain, and put it back in the sky. Across the world they saw his silhouette, but only those from his home town recognized him. Everyone else just called him Light Bringer. The anonymous legend."

A silhouette against the sky. Just like Tanner at the top of the staircase. Had he known the story? Had he brought me there, at that time, to show me that?

We walked for another few minutes, then Fitz hazarded a question, "Do you have a hero name?"

I shook my head, "Maybe we can pick one on the way."

There would be plenty of time. When we got outside the palace, Tanner jogged over. The bags the attendants had packed us were bouncing on his back, and his pockets clinked suspiciously.

He recited all the information Kingsman's researchers had given him.

We'd leave the city and head for a small town halfway between us and the army. Kingsman's men were already working on clearing the city, and the army was going to start their march that way soon.

There were several large mills there. We'd get Fitz to the top, where he could play and the whole army could see him. This was the objective, and the end goal if Daemon wasn't there. If he was, we'd separate him, and we'd take him, in a hypnotized state, back to the capital, where they'd twist his arm into disbanding the theocracy of his cult.

Tanner's role, similar to the last mission, was to keep the piper–Fitz–and I alive. I was the insurance policy in case he failed, but we weren't expecting much resistance.

The secret role we'd play would be to keep Fitz in line, make sure he didn't start possessing anyone else for example.

It wouldn't be a difficult mission, or a large one, but Kingsman had accepted it for us because it would be risky, and no adults would be safe on the trip. Of course they could always wear ear plugs, but that left them deaf to many warning signs of armies, or ambushes, or cries for help.

We set off that night. We had been given instructions to get the piper out of the city as quickly as possible, so we left through our secret entrance. We had to loop back to the main road, but it protected the city from the danger that the piper would start trying to control them.

I wasn't nearly as wary of that as I had been. I had several different logical excuses for my trust, but to tell the truth, the real reason I trusted him was his smile. It seemed impossible for someone to fake such an unassuming thing. He had seemed timid, which had made me consider that he'd do something stupid out of fear, but he wasn't always timid, something I learned fast.

Still, I wasn't trusting enough to wait in the city for Ginger and Joey. Instead we waited on the main road out of the capital. Soon enough Ginger and Joey appeared from opposite ends of the wall. Joey had taken a secret passage under the wall, exclusively for noble use. There was a gap in the grate that the Wide River flowed through, and Ginger had swum through. She wasn't even

188

sodden when she reached us though, because she'd made more matter confusion potions, and the water had turned to air and let her crawl through.

"I brought goodies," Tanner said, pulling a collection of items from his pockets. There were two small crumpled sacs in case they hadn't brought their own–they had–and dozens of important but tiny items. He had stuffed a few pouches of jerky bits into his pockets, thin daggers had been tucked into his boots, extra rope was tied around his waist, and two canisters for water were hidden under his shirt.

He distributed the goods to Joey and Ginger who, thankfully, had prepared their own supplies as well.

Ginger met Fitz with her characteristic charisma, and quickly realized Fitz had the mind of a poet. He thought the entire world was telling a story, and he had all the words to interpret it. I supposed he talked so much because all those thoughts and metaphors had been in his head for years. She was content to listen to him talk about it, adding her own more romantic thoughts to the mix.

Joey was stiff, as he always was at first, but made some attempts to connect with Fitz. He taught him about the flute, and gave him a basic rundown of the notes and how it ought to be played.

Tanner and Fitz got along like the house on fire. Tanner was entertained by Fitz's comments, and it only took a few hours of walking to discover they had the exact same sense of humor. Their conversation came so easily I rarely had the opportunity to jump in, and when I did I felt more like I was interrupting than an actual member of the conversation. Not to mention, Fitz called me Edy. I couldn't exactly tell him I hated that nickname, because he seemed to believe that using a nickname was what meant we were friends.

And we were. In an odd way. It was the kind of friendship that seemed like a fever dream. Had we ever really spoken, or was it all said by the way he moved? Were we friends because he had no knowledge of what to look for in friends, or because he truly enjoyed my company?

I definitely felt more distant from Fitz than Tanner and Ginger did–perhaps even more than Joey. Maybe it was because I tried to keep in mind that I couldn't get too attached because I may have to murder him at some approaching time. Maybe it was because I just didn't make friends easily. Maybe–and this was the hardest to admit to myself–it was because I wished I was more like him.

His motivation seemed so pure. He'd accepted us immediately and started sharing so much. It was like he trusted us completely. Still, he wasn't weak. He was somehow vulnerable and powerful. He seemed shocked every time we offered him the most basic kinds of kindness, reaching out to keep him from tripping off cliffs, helping him roll out his cot and tie up his tent– something we'd actually been taught by one of the palace officials so we wouldn't set anything on fire again.

The reason is besides the point, I suppose. It didn't matter why we didn't connect, it didn't really matter how we got along. All that mattered was getting him to the mill quickly.

Luckily no one died along the way. Last time we'd known the trip would've been more enjoyable if we had a poet to make conversation. This time we had one, and the time passed much more enjoyably. We met less with agents–Ginger was very disappointed that Tog never appeared–and traveled more at night to avoid the rising heat.

Less luckily, we never made it to the mill. Daemon's army had been moving faster than anyone had anticipated.

We'd woken before the sun on the morning we found them. When the sun had finally risen enough to spear the mist with its rays, it revealed the dust of hundreds of moving bodies on the horizon.

"That can't be the army can it?" Tanner's voice was taut with disbelief.

"Holy…" Ginger trailed off, one hand raised to block the sunlight from her eyes.

I squinted and tried to determine for sure who it was.

"It could be the evacuating townspeople," I theorized, but I wasn't hopeful. The sinking in my stomach told me it was the army, and we weren't in position.

I squeezed my lucky gemstone.

"It's the army. Do you hear the footsteps?" Fitz's voice shook.

I listened closely. Instead of the roar of hundreds of feet, there was a discernable pattern.

"Are they running in sync?" Tanner asked incredulously.

Fitz nodded, "They all are obeying the same orders."

"Interesting. Do they always act in such accordance?" Joey shuffled through his pack to find one of his notebooks.

"Yes," Fitz replied simply. This time when his voice wasn't quiet, it wasn't a powerful quiet. It was a scared quiet.

I looked around frantically. We'd been climbing hills for a while, but the past few days the landscape had been entirely flat. The only high ground in sight were the mountains, and they were hazy in the distance. There weren't even any trees, only small brush livened up the drab plains.

This was not happening.

"What are we going to do?" I asked. I sounded so afraid it almost made me sick.

Ginger squeezed my shoulder comfortingly, "We have time to come up with something."

"They can't keep up a flat run like that for very long," Tanner said, then looked at Fitz, "right?"

"I don't know. We always walked."

This wasn't the plan. We were going to take control of the entire army with a flute. We couldn't do that if no one could hear the music.

"You were in control before, can you possess them without music?" this time I was careful to keep my fear out of my voice. I knew my friends weren't fooled. They'd notice how I gnawed on my lip, how I ran a hand through my hair as I stared down the army.

Fitz shook his head, "I've been out of view. I can't control them mentally until I play again."

192

I clenched my jaw and tried to think.

With how loud their footsteps were, very few people would even hear the music.

"It's likely they're on orders to run straight to the capital. They may not slow, but they probably wouldn't attack, if the objective is speed," Joey paused, "Though I suppose…do you remember the slogan of the Red Rebellion?"

I immediately answered, "Move or perish." Joey had told me that before, although I couldn't remember when. It had originated when a town militia had tried to stop Daemon's men from moving out, and Daemon said that if they didn't get out of the way, they'd run them through. The militia hadn't moved. They'd all been slain.

Ginger swallowed, "They may not have the same perspective this time."

We all were looking at Joey, and at the back of my mind I recognized how much pressure we were putting on him. We wanted him to give us the answers.

That hope, that he'd know, that he could somehow fix it, made it all the more terrifying when Joey shook his head.

That movement made my heart drop into my stomach. They wouldn't pass us by.

"We probably have a few hours before they reach us. Anyone have any brilliant ideas?" Tanner was already digging through his pack to find anything useful.

"This wasn't the plan." I mutter, dropping to my knees to copy him, digging through my pack to find anything I could use.

"We aren't dead yet." Tanner said grimly.

Fitz had played the flute a small amount as we walked, learning how to make the different notes, and inventing simple melodies. Like his poetry, the songs were thick with emotion, every note striking some chord inside me.

This time he raised it to his lips to calm himself. The tune he played was fast. He left the notes no time to hang in the air before he covered them with the next few. It might have been calming him down, but it only stressed me out more.

I knew, mentally, that we had hours and there was no need to panic yet. Physically, I knew something completely different. My heart, my lungs, the adrenaline in my ears, it all told me I was going to die.

Ginger was pulling carefully wrapped vials from her pack and started arranging them on the dusty ground.

Tanner started spitballing ideas, "We could make a tower out of tent poles."

"It wouldn't be sturdy enough," I discouraged.

"We could attract their attention and try to draw them all the way to the village with the mill?"

"We couldn't keep ahead of them, even if they did follow us," This time Joey was the discouraging voice.

"They would follow us," Tanner said, "with your red cloak they couldn't lose us."

"It's like a matador in a ring," Fitz affirmed, "they'd see the red and run for it."

My nerves were already frazzled. I'd spent days traveling with one of my friends, and struggling with the idea that I may

194

have to kill his newer, and apparently better, friend. I hadn't been eating enough, because I knew Fitz had never had enough, and teenage boys ate so much.

The biggest problem? I didn't have time to make traps, and that's what I did. Besides reviving people, I made traps, and traps always were planned. The inputs always created the same outputs. Pull a rope and men swing into a tree. Tug a chord and potion bottles break. Play a tune and control an army. Our plan had fallen to pieces, and we had just the wrong amount of time; not enough to prepare, too much to run on adrenaline.

All these factors combined into one horrible emotional stew, so Tanner and Fitz's attempts to come up with a plan felt more like they were ganging up on me.

"It's a fine idea except for the fact that the possessed army can probably run as fast as humanly possible without stopping. Even if they follow us, they'd catch up and kill us," I spat, "Not to mention, the village is past them. We'd have to somehow make a giant loop to keep them from trampling us."

Ginger and Joey were both absorbed in their own thoughts, Joey was frantically scribbling in his notebook, and Ginger was muttering the uses of each of her potions.

Tanner tipped back on his heels, his hands stilling, "So what do you suggest Edy? We sit here and wait for them to kill us?" The sardonic tone did nothing to make me calm down, nor did the annoyed look he leveled my way.

"...healing, agility..."

"I'm just trying to be practical!"

"Yeah. You're doing great. Do you think you can offer practical solutions?" Tanner made a curt gesture, and a beam of light glanced off his ring and into my eyes.

"...bone growth, clarity..."

My hands paused in their search, clenching around whatever was in my fists. It dug into my palms until pain radiated from them but it barely registered.

Fitz had retreated inside himself, the way he did when he was unsure or uncomfortable. His shoulders hunched forward, his arms crossed over his chest. It was a subconscious attempt to make himself smaller, and to protect his heart and wrists from attack.

I bit my tongue so hard it drew blood, but I tried to calm down. Anger wasn't productive. My attempt was nearly useless. My vision had narrowed, and my arms were shaking with restrained energy.

I forced my fingers to relaz slightly, and some of the gemstones I'd been gripping so tightly clattered from my hands.

I looked down and started rooting through my bag again. Angry tears had threatened to make an appearance, and I wouldn't let Tanner, or the others for that matter, see them.

"Great. Now you're mad at me." Tanner muttered, continuing to root through his bag.

I searched through the gemstones with my fingers, trying to focus only on the physical sensation. I had to calm down. I had to think.

When I felt the right stone, I raised it from the bag. Apparently I'd clutched the stones tighter than I'd even

196

recognized, because my palm glistened from a dozen tiny cuts. The stone I held was enchanted with comforting. I pressed it into my palm as I kept digging with my other hand.

Ginger looked up from her collection, "Guys! Clarity! Let's all have some clarity!" She held up a tiny vial full of green liquid.

Joey was pulled from his notebook to look up at the vial, and its small portions.

"There isn't enough for all of us. Who should take it?" Tanner grabbed the vial, and tilted it this way and that, looking through the glistening liquid.

"Joey ought to take it," Ginger said, glancing around the circle. My face was still set in anger, which had nothing to do with her, but just in case she added, "no offense to anyone else, but he is kind of the smart one."

Tanner nodded and tossed the vial to Joey. Despite Joey's trained athleticism, his hands were full of a pen and notebook, and he was too late. The vial curved through the air and broke against his chest.

Tanner's mouth fell open, and Ginger squeaked, "it may still work when it's applied topically?"

I tightened my fist around the comforting gemstone, but its effects seemed to be weakening.

"Does anyone have any other ideas?" My throat was tight and the words had to push their way through my unyielding lips.

Ginger's eyes were wide with a kind of worry as she looked at each of us in turn, "Fitz you look like you have an idea. Anything is helpful."

"They might hear me playing when they get close, even though there are a lot of them. Maybe I can start a chain reaction? Make the ones who hear humm my tune so the others are caught?"

"That could work," Ginger affirmed, "Don't you think Joey?"

Joey listed his head to the side, "I suppose I'm not sure. It could work. The enchantment is limited so there's a possibility it won't work but…"

"But it's still worth a try," Ginger finished.

I tightened my fist even harder around the gemstone, and I squeezed my eyes shut. A solitary tear fell down my face as I tried to feel comforted. It felt so useless, all this last minute planning.

Tanner was staring at me, and something in the way he gritted his teeth reminded me I hadn't suggested any brilliant solutions yet. For a pair of thieves, we were surprisingly horrible under pressure, and the adrenaline had turned to venom in both of us, making us unreasonably angry with the whole thing.

"Any thoughts Edy?" His tone was caustic, but he was talking in the quiet judgemental way he had.

I looked up at him, and hoped the tear hadn't left a track, "None. Fitz seems to have it all figured out."

Fitz shrunk away from me, and I felt a twinge. I hadn't meant to insult him.

Tanner noticed Fitz's reaction, and he scoffed at me, "that's what it is huh? You feel threatened because Fitz is cleverer than you?"

I tried to understand that Tanner was just angry at the

situation. He was angry the same way I was angry. I knew that, but it didn't help.

"That's great Tanner. Belittle me. That's really helpful," I said.

At the same time Ginger scolded both of us, "Leave Fitz out of your spat. He's being helpful."

I cinched the top of my pack closed and stood up, flicking my cloak so it snapped around me.

"What are you going to do? Run away?" Tanner sneered.

"Not helpful Tanner," Ginger said.

"Why do you sound so derisive?" I said mordantly, looking over Ginger to look down at Tanner "that's what you wanted me to do a minute ago. With my red cape they'd all follow me, and as they run by trying to kill me, you can charm them."

"You know that's not what he meant," Ginger said peaceably.

"Maybe that is what I meant, I mean, since you don't seem of use otherwise," Tanner raised his chin, almost as a challenge.

"Right. But as far as practical solutions go, I'd say it's effective. When they finally catch up with me you'll have time to get them all while they tear me apart."

Joey raised his hands, as if he was finally preparing himself to help mediate the conflict. Ginger was trying to find a potion that might calm us down. Fitz's expression was bent with sorrow–I guess it was disappointing to see his heroes so unheroic.

Tanner stood up to face me, but I turned away.

I stalked several paces away and started to assemble a base from the wooden tent poles that were in my pack.

"Oh so now you like the idea of a tower?"

Ginger looked ready to wrestle Tanner to the ground, "be the bigger person here Tanner. Stop antagonizing Kennedy."

I ignored them and placed the next pole.

"We'll need to find more wood. Can you find some logs? Hit them my way with that ring?" I cast Tanner a glance over my shoulder. He bristled at my dismissive tone.

I turned to Fitz, and tried to keep my voice perfectly normal, "Your chain reaction idea isn't bad. Are you willing to get on this tower and play?"

Fitz straightened his back and tried to project confidence when he said, "Of course."

"When the army was with you, they weren't armed were they?"

"No."

"Good, then they won't have arrows to shoot you. Maybe we can puzzle their zombie brains with a tower."

"They'll probably be able to knock it over or climb it," Tanner said.

"Thanks for your constructive criticism," I quipped, "we can stand at the top of the tower as they approach. They won't miss us when I'm wearing my red cloak. When they get close, Fitz will play. They won't get close enough to so much as touch the tower."

Tanner opened his mouth to say something else, but I cut him off, "Have you found any logs yet?"

In the end, the tower wasn't really a tower. It was a glorified step stool, standing at only five or so feet tall. We'd dragged over

a few fallen logs, but there weren't enough to make the structure
sturdy. It could barely hold Fitz weight, and he was the thinnest
of us. The wood was bent together in a strange configuration that
somehow reminded me of a hand, reaching up from the ground
and holding Fitz in its palm. We built up mounds of dirt around
the poles at the base so they'd be stable, and we found the thickest
branches of the nearby brush and built them into the structure
as well. Rope strung it all together, and it didn't instill much
confidence that twine could make the difference between life
and death. In the end it was a hazard of splinters and stabs barely
hanging together, but it would work.

The army was still at least an hour away when the tower was
complete, so we grabbed everything useful and stuffed our bags
into the brush in the structure, where we hoped they wouldn't be
trampled.

Ginger distributed agility and strength potions, offering Fitz
a healing potion in case something went wrong, and giving me all
the indivisible bottles. I knew it was because it was important for
me to survive, but it felt like just another affront.

Joey charted the plan of attack, in case anyone passed the
musical barrier. We'd all stand along the front, and incapacitate
anyone who came too close. If they started to surround us, we'd
each take separate corners and defend our space as best we could,
keeping our backs to the tower at all times.

We had worked mostly in silence, with occasional melodies
added by Fitz. After we'd finished dinner and the fire was starting
to die, I decided I was calm enough to apologize to Tanner,

although I still felt the need to clutch the comforting gemstone in my hand.

I sat beside him, and he stabbed the fire with his makeshift poker a little harder than necessary.

"I'm sorry I got so frustrated."

Tanner poked at the fire a little more.

"Your ideas were good. I just…I was antagonizing because I was scared. I shouldn't have taken it out on you."

Tanner looked up, but not at me, "I accept your apology."

When he didn't say anything else, I moved to stand, give him some space until I thought he could tolerate me again.

"I don't really think you're useless," he said, "just stay here for a minute."

I sat back down.

Across the fire, Fitz raised his flute and started to play a simple nursery rhyme. If I remembered correctly, it was a rhyme about the way fire has a soul.

Ginger remembered the rhyme better than I did, and even did the hand motions to accompany the song. Joey watched the fire with a strange fervor, like it held all the answers.

I smiled to myself and thought that if we made it out alive, I'd have to ask Fitz to teach me to play.

"I'm scared too," Tanner said quietly, "I think you've rubbed off on me."

I leaned in to bump his shoulder, and I lingered a second longer than necessary, appreciating his warmth.

We sat there in companionable silence until the army was

close enough to scare all of us to our tower.

We stamped out the embers of the fire, and I handed my cloak to Fitz. He would be the only one on the tower, so we figured he should be the visible one.

Most of our plan depended on him, so we had to make sure to keep him safe.

We all gripped potions fast in our hands, Tanner had his strength ring, and I had my lucky jewel. Ginger and I both held two daggers, and Joey and Tanner had their swords, but they seemed more flimsy than the enchantments. Probably because we could imagine the enchanted things to be so much more powerful, and we knew the limitations of metal.

"You good up there?" Tanner called.

"All set," Fitz called down.

I knew he was terrified. We all were. More than that, I knew he was excited. After years of living as a shadow, he was able to do something great. He was going to stop an army, save a kingdom. Of course, he had created the army in the first place, but that's what made it so much more powerful. He was overcoming more than an army, he was overcoming himself.

The army was still a little ways off, but the sheer number of people hadn't struck me until just then. I had no comprehension of the size of an army, because I'd never seen this many people together. I tried to keep up my hope as they neared, but there were so many of them. Their footsteps, all in eerie sync, shook the ground as if a giant was running toward us.

The dirt we'd piled up around the tower supports began to

shake and miniature avalanches of dirt slid from the tops.

The blood had mostly withdrawn from my fingers and they became cold and shaky. That's not a good combination when all that was between me and a horde of people was a small pair of knives, held in those shaking and cold fingers.

I nearly sliced my toes off dropping my knives as we waited.

"It'll be fine," Ginger reassured unconvincingly, "no one will even reach us."

Except they would. I knew they would, because the pounding of their feet was loud enough Ginger had to raise her voice and no flute had that volume. No flute could be that loud. They'd storm toward us and without so much as a pause, they'd trample us and the tower and we'd be dead and the king would die and I'd never said goodbye to my family. Why hadn't I stopped to say goodbye? Why hadn't I chosen a different mission?

The footsteps were getting louder. Boom boom boom boom.

This was the most terrified I'd ever been, and that terror built in me like a wave, pounding against my defenses, making my brain turn to mush and my breathing into ragged gasps like sobs.

Boom boom boom boom.

The sun was heavy on the mountains like a dew drop, and I knew that soon it would dip below the horizon and everything would go dark—boom boom boom boom—and I wouldn't even know who I was stabbing or if the blood was my own or if I was dying and the world was going black for real. Boom boom boom boom.

Tanner must've seen something of my frantic thoughts,

because he sheathed his sword and put his hands on my shoulders and turned me to face him.

They were cold and managed to shock my thoughts to a standstill.

"We've got this ok!" He was yelling but I still barely heard him.

Boom boom boom boom.

"I don't want to die," I cried, but he didn't hear me.

Boom boom boom boom.

"I've got your back Edy."

Only when he let go and turned back to look at the army did I realize how much I was fidgeting. Fidgeting and twitching. I wasn't sure whether it was nerves or cold, but I couldn't stop moving. Ginger was the same, and Tanner was agitated, but Joey stood as still and sure as a mountain.

Boom boom boom boom.

It was time for Fitz to start playing. Was he playing? I couldn't hear it.

Boom boom boom boom.

Heavens it was time for him to play and if I couldn't hear it the army wouldn't either I was going to be stampeded to death– boom boom boom boom–the King had been right teenagers were foolish. Why had I agreed to this? Why had I done this? To be a legend? What use was that if I didn't survive to revel in it?

Boom boom boom boom.

The army was getting close enough I could see features of individual members. I was going to die.

Boom boom boom boom.

No. I was fine. We got this. I was a necromancer for heaven's sake. I robbed the King himself. I survived an attack from a cultist when I was unarmed. We took down senior members of Befreiung der Verdammten during a surprise attack. I was not going to let myself die because of panic.

Boom boom boom boom.

My steely resolve sent ice running through my veins, stabilizing my hands, calming my nerves. We got this.

The sunset was beautiful over the heads of the enemy. All shades of reds and golds.

A clear note rang through the air, and it was the same warm comforting color.

Boom boom boom boom.

The men were fifty feet away. Twenty-five. Fifteen. Their momentum carried them to within ten feet of the tower, before they fell out of sync with those behind them, and began to hum.

Their collective voices filled the night with a powerful sound, and those humming turned around to push against the others still trying to get forward and hummed at them.

An unbelieving laugh bubbled up from my chest. This was working! We might not even need to fight!

That hope was the melody Fitz played. That hope was the tune that filled the night, strengthened by a hundred voices.

Yet, there was no ripple. There was no chain reaction, somewhere along the line, a link had broken and the signal wasn't getting across.

The people pressing towards us did not stop. They pushed those who were humming back, and began to spill around, until we stood at the center of a very large ring, and a very thin number of people were trying to stop them from crushing in.

Joey gave the signal and we separated, Joey and Ginger stepping sideways to the other corners of the tower.

How many of them were there? A thousand? Ten thousand?

In fact, those who were pushing in were getting closer. The humming drowned out the sound of the flute even more than their marching had.

"Stop the humming," I screamed, but the air swallowed up my voice and the humming continued. No longer the sound of sunset, it sounded like damnation.

A humming man was trampled, and a woman with a face as blank and smooth as river rock raced toward me. Fitz must've faltered in panic, because the high clear notes trailed off for a mere instant, long enough for her to reach me without hearing it.

I raised my blade, and found I had to do nothing more. She didn't pause. She didn't raise her hands to defend herself. She ran right into the knife, and I felt it sink into her. It didn't deter her. She kept moving toward me, even as the knife plunged deeper into her gut. Her bland expression didn't even flicker.

As her momentum and force threatened to tip me backwards, I sliced her throat with my other dagger. Something warm and sticky splattered my forehead. The woman slid off my knife.

I looked in horror at the knives in my hands, crimson streaming off the blades and dripping down my arms to my elbows.

I didn't have much time to panic, because there were more blank eyed, blank faced attackers rushing towards me.

The melody lost its hope. An echo of my mind.

I stabbed the next man between his ribs, knowing full well he wouldn't try to stop me. The knife slid in. The knife slid out.

I downed the strength potion to stop the shaking in my limbs.

A young adult bumped into my side and nearly knocked me over. I targeted their neck.

More and more of them were surrounding me. Soon the air was thick with the scent of death. The earth was becoming muddy. And corpses were as abundant as the brush.

It sounded broken. Synchronized footsteps in two different rhythms, disjointed humming, somewhere a piercing whistle. My breathing sounded unnaturally loud in my own ears, even when the adrenaline drowned out the sound. There were no screams, no shouts, besides our own.

It turns out it's not difficult to kill someone who's not fighting back. Physically, I mean. Even in my cold, starving, and terrified state, I was knocking enemies to the ground in droves.

Mentally it was the hardest thing I think I've ever done. I stopped thinking of them as people, that was the only way I could handle it. They were drones, zombies, buggers, anything but human. It twisted things to view it that way, and I wondered absently if anything would ever be the way it was.

I realized then, in a poorly timed epiphany, that the blank stone the cultist had given me was denial. When everything was in its place, but it was all off. It hadn't been written on the stone because to be true denial it couldn't be named. In my case it wasn't true denial, it was the forced distancing of myself from the nightmare I was living.

They threw themselves at me, onto my blades. Their blank expressions were identical. It seemed I was fighting a hydra, and everytime I cut a neck, another two sprouted up.

They were aggressive, but their only attack was to ram into me. It wasn't that threatening at first. Fitz's people pushed them away, and kept them from attacking in large numbers.

The sun hadn't fully set, lingering just on the precipice. It mocked me, the golds and pinks that had been warmth turned to red. The color of a harsh reality.

I stabbed blindly as the sun began to slip. I fought as it sank just below. I raged as it disappeared. I danced as its last rays vanished.

I saw Ginger swimming over the army, but after another corpse slipped off my knife I couldn't find her.

My energy was dissipating, but I'd gotten the hang of it. Stab, slice, slip. Stab, slice, slip. A shell hit my back and after a stumble I turned to face it. Stab, slice, slip.

A monster. Stab, slice, slip.

A demon. Stab, slice, slip.

A hollow. Stab, slice, slip.

It became a mantra. Repeating in my head endlessly.

There was music coming from somewhere. It was high and sharp and pricked my eardrums. Someone was screaming.

Stab slice slip.

A burly one fell into me, pushed by those behind him. Even as my knife embedded in his chest I tripped backwards and my head hit a log in the tower.

I hit the ground and the man landed on top of me, forcing all the air from my lungs. Stars burst behind my eyes, but I knew the zombies would be closing in.

I tried to stand up but my legs were trapped beneath an immense weight and the strength potion had worn off. A boot landed hard on my chest, and I felt something snap. I sliced blindly at the heel, and the bugger crumpled. I coughed, and blood filled my mouth.

"That's not good," I mumbled, and I kicked the body off my legs. The effort seemed to take all my adrenaline, and before I could stand more bogeymen were running across my body, stamping on my face.

Then they were gone, and someone was pulling me up by the arm.

I swayed on my feet when I was upright. I was missing a knife, it was probably still in the burly one.

I turned toward the hand that had helped me up, and was almost shocked to see a face that wasn't empty.

My hand was raised for the first step, stab, but I stopped.

"Edy are you ok?" the person roared.

I blinked. Edy. Who was that?

A rabid thing was coming toward my side. Stab, slice, slip.

The real one turned my face to look it in the eye.

"Kennedy! Are you ok?!"

Kennedy. That was my name.

I blinked, "Tanner?"

"Yes Edy it's me! Are you ok?"

Sudden nausea hit me like a cannonball, and I stumbled backward, clutching at my stomach.

I ran into a shadow, and they tried to push me over. I turned to face them, and saw that they had a face. A hollow one, but they were not a shadow.

It happened just like that. Denial stabslices*slipped* away from me. That was a person. A person with blond hair that was white in the moonlight. A person with thin lips and a button nose. A person with extraordinary small ears.

A sword reached over my shoulder and impaled the blond person.

I screamed.

Tanner shoved me back against the tower, and started sweeping widely with his sword. He was lucky. It was long and the blood didn't drip down his wrists.

I stopped myself there. That wasn't lucky.

"Stay back," Tanner shouted, beheading a human being with a powerful slice.

"I can't" I said. It was true. I couldn't do this. We hadn't killed more than a fraction of them. We had killed a fraction of them.

Is this what was waiting for the kingdom? The moral people get trampled to death, and the rest end up madmen.

Tanner kept attacking, but my vision was going blurry and strange. The world was undulating from my exhaustion.

I had the function of mind to wonder where Joey and Ginger were, and I couldn't spot them through my hazy vision.

Tanner shouted that I couldn't black out. Black out. Black was a color. So was red. Red was blood. Blood was life. Life was pain. Pain was terror. Terror was red. Red was blood. Blood was death. Death was terror. Terror was red.

I shook my head to stop the repeating, but what I could see was worse.

The sky was black. The stars were blue. The stars were also white. The stars were also red. Red was blood. Blood was pain.

I covered my ears but the voice was in my head.

Pain was terror. Hope was death. Life was a dream.

Inspiration was a silver ring.

A silver ring punched forward, throwing an opponent back. A silver ring. A strength ring.

I grabbed Tanner's non-sword arm, and he looked back at me curiously. I straightened out his fingers from their fist, and I pulled the ring off.

He tried to curl his fingers to stop me, but he was too late.

"You aren't fighting in your state! Give me back the ring!" Tanner yelled.

"Fitz needs it" I yelled back, deliriously proud of remembering his name. Tanner looked at me, and in the length of time it took for him to understand, someone knocked him to the ground. I didn't have my knife, and I wasn't wearing the strength

212

ring. I tried to shove the people bodily away from Tanner, but then there was the threat that I would fall, and that couldn't happen.

Silver is inspiration. Inspiration is strength.

I turned away from the trampling herd and climbed the tower. It wasn't much of a tower. Only five feet high. Splinters stabbed my hands. The crowd didn't try to tear me down. They didn't know how. They just pounded into me as I climbed.

I reached the top, where Fitz was playing with his eyes squeezed shut. Tears had washed his cheeks clean of dirt, and my cloak whipped around him.

He was playing a song, I was now close enough to hear. A song so sorrowful the night seemed shades of blue, even when I knew it was scarlet.

I stood up, and nearly fell off when the tower wobbled.

Fitz's eyes popped open in alarm, and when he saw me he stopped playing and gaped open mouthed and sobbing at me. I supposed I looked like a monster. A demon. Not a hero, not a legend.

I took hold of his flute, and he let me. The horde below was shuffling against the tower, their heads level with its top. It wobbled, but didn't fall yet.

I slid the strength ring onto the stalk of the flute, and handed it back to Fitz. Understanding gleamed in his eyes. Or maybe they were tears.

He closed his eyes, and when he played the sound broke the sky into a thousand shards of starry glass.

Every sound was silenced at once. The crowd stopped

moving.

The music wasn't loud enough it hurt. In fact it was a whisper. A whisper like the end of a bed tale. A whisper like the last line of a tragedy. A whisper like a secret.

But it was strong. It swirled through the night like a ballet dancer. It didn't trip, it didn't stumble.

Fitz opened his eyes as the last note played. Every pair of eyes was focused on him.

He made no physical gesture, but the throng moved back, leaving a large circle around the tower.

He nodded at me, and we both climbed numbly down from the top.

Fitz cried out when he saw the ground, covered as it was with the fallen.

I told him to have the army lay out the dead.

He looked at me blankly.

I reminded him I was Edy. I was a necromancer.

He understood then, and the empty faces of hundreds stepped around me and carefully carried the fallen to empty ground, arranging their bodies in perfect order.

We had been efficient, and people were strewn about the tower. The army itself had been more lethal, trampling the others who tried to resist.

There were uncountable dead. And not just uncountable because I was uneducated. There were so many that the earth seemed more skin and blood than dirt and brush.

The army made neat rows of the bodies, and lined up the

limbs just so. I ignored every soul, searching only for the three I knew were missing.

Tanner was the first, and I almost missed him, because he didn't look like Tanner.

Red is blood. Blood is pain. Pain is terror.

I told my head to stop. It didn't, but it only spoke quieter.

I knelt down, and made sure he was put together right. Then I poked him back to life.

Chapter 15
Kennedy

Joey was only a few people to Tanner's left. I checked the way he was laid out, then brought him back. Ginger was a few rows down, and was the worst of the three. Her legs were entirely bent out of order, and the army had failed to straighten them correctly. I did so, and brought her back.

I spent the entire night trailing along the rows. It would have been quicker to walk in a hunch, letting my fingertips brush the people's bodies and bring them back, but I knew the army hadn't put them together right. So, I stepped in front of each crumpled and broken body, and I fixed them. There were so many, but the work never became routine, for each revival was a new reminder of the tragedy, every person had their own figure and their own injuries.

Daemon John wasn't among them, or the survivors. Apparently he'd sent his army toward the King and gone a different way himself.

I had been afraid, when I brought back the first–after Tanner and Joey and Ginger. Afraid Fitz's power would count as a curse. Afraid I wouldn't survive more exhaustion. I stood over that first person for what felt like hours. They had golden hair that had lost its luster to the dust. They had a large nose, but an elegant one. Thin lips. High cheekbones. They laid there so neatly, it was almost like they were sleeping, almost like I couldn't even notice the gash over their heart.

I leaned over and closed their eyes.

The change began that instant, their skin peeling and being replaced, their internal anatomy writing back into place.

I stumbled back, but realized quickly that it was because bending over had made me dizzy, and not because the curse registered.

It didn't tire me at all. So I kept going.

Fitz tried to stop me, tried to tell me to rest, but I told him death was terror and these people had already been through enough of that. Fitz let me keep going.

After a time sitting by the tower, Tanner came over and started to help, arranging the bodies before I could get there. There was pain in his posture, even though I knew he was physically healed.

I could ask if he'd rather be dead. Stab, slice, slip.

I didn't want to know the answer, so I never did.

Joey and Ginger started helping too, gritting their teeth at the horror, their only relief being the fact that none of the carnage was enduring.

The revived ones were back to themselves. They had no memory of dying, no memory of their trip from whatever town they'd been found in. I never answered their questions, and they seemed to know not to interrupt Ginger, Joey, and Tanner in their work. Fitz got tired of repeating the same story, so he made the army do it. One long repeating chorus.

The sun rose on muddy plains, and I paused in my work to drink in the brilliant yellow-white color. It was not the color of pain. It was the color of purity, the color of truth, and the color of hope.

When I finished the resurrections, we all gathered together around the tower.

At one point the army's chorus changed, then broke off into disjointed muttering. Somehow Fitz arranged those who'd heard the chorus into the crowd, and they explained what had happened to the others, and then they all started to walk.

I wasn't sure where they were walking. Probably home. I didn't know where they'd be getting food or water. I hoped someone would bring me anyone who passed away. Except they didn't know my name.

When Fitz seemed satisfied with the emptiness of the plains, he walked and joined us by the tower.

"The sky is pretty today," he said softly.

We all tipped our chins back to look at it. It was the same blue as the painting at the palace. The shade of blue Ginger said looked like love.

"It's a gentle color. And it covers us so neatly. Just imagine,

218

if we'd had a different god, the sky may have a seam. Not with this god though. We have a smooth sky."

"Told you things were better with a poet around," Ginger said.

And she was right. Fitz made the trip back much more enjoyable with his little observances and comments. We even laughed a few times.

When we reached the city, Joey took us through the noble's secret entrance.

There were still sounds, in the dead of night. They were natural sounding sounds. Unlike the army.

There was peace in them.

I caught Tanner looking at me. He looked away when I looked at him. I wanted to say something but I didn't know what to say.

We reached the palace gates, and the guards let us in. They escorted us into the palace, and when Marie appeared she visibly recoiled from the amount of dirt we tracked in.

She called more servants, and they prepared baths for us.

When I was being led away, she asked what had happened.

I wanted to keep it simple, tell her we stopped the army, but I couldn't.

"All the people from the eastern towns caught up with us on the plains. We couldn't release them from their possession fast enough, and there was a massacre," my voice didn't sound like my own, so I cleared my throat, "we made sure to bring them all back. They're going home."

She looked at my blood stained clothing, and the blood crusted under my fingernails.

"Thank you for saving us, and them." Her face had the maternal look again, "We'll bring you new clothes. And… Kennedy have you ever painted your nails?"

I shook my head, and she said I could pick the colors.

Ginger got the same options.

That was odd. I'd never heard of painting nails. Would it be permanent?

The bath was full of steaming water. It gave me the impression that my skin was being purified. Flakes of red drifted to the top, and I used a horse hair brush to scrub my skin raw. When I dunked my hair, I was surprised by how it dyed the water.

I got out quickly after that, and found a pair of neatly folded clothes near the door. They smelled like flowers, and I felt sorry for how many had to be crushed for the small amount of fragrance.

I left the room, and two maids and Ginger were standing right outside. The maids told us we could choose yellow, blue, red, or purple.

Ginger picked blue, but I chose yellow. It was the color of hope, the color of the sun rising after a dark night.

They took us into a room, and held our hands flat on the desk. One of them painted my nails with a long paint brush with short bristles. The other combed my hair, and tied it in a knot at the top of my head. It felt heavy, but I'm sure Ginger's was worse, because her knot piled much higher than mine.

"I feel like a noble," Ginger said, admiring her drying nails.

220

"Why? Does Joey paint his nails?"

Ginger shrugged, "If he doesn't we should get him to. I'm sure his sisters would love it too."

The maids led us from the room, and another servant escorted me up to a set of familiar halls. Tanner and Joey met us there. I'd forgotten how pale of a brown Tanner's hair was. It was always dirty and looked several shades darker.

"They gave you new clothes too," I said.

Tanner nodded, "Do I look like a noble?"

I contemplated that for a second, "Nope. Your nails aren't painted," I raised mine to show them off.

"Fair point," he looked at Joey, "Joey you don't look like a noble."

Joey shrugged, "I've never seen paint as the identifying factor."

Ginger's eyes twinkled, "Oh but it should be. The lower classes couldn't afford something so frivolous, so it makes you stand out."

Tanner raised his hands in a pompous attempt to get them to shut up, "Ladies and gentlemen, there's no need to fight. None of us look like nobles."

We all laughed, "We look like a Joey, a Ginger, a Tanner, and a Kennedy" I said.

"You mean an Edy," Tanner corrected.

"I don't mind that name anymore," I realized.

Tanner grinned, "That takes all the fun out of it."

Fitz joined us when we arrived at the waiting chambers

beside Kingsman's rooms.

He was clean for maybe the first time in his life. The vitiligo that had earned him the name Pied Piper was more clear than I'd seen it. It was beautiful.

"Nice to see you Fitz," Tanner said, stepping forward to give him a hug.

"You saw me just a minute ago," Fitz said.

"But I've never seen you clean," Tanner teased, "You look like a whole different person."

Kingsman peered around the doorframe, "You all made it back," he paused a beat, "Ginger, Joey, I don't think you two were invited."

"We decided stopping an army was a five person job," Ginger quipped.

Kingsman shrugged, "Fair enough. I can't exactly punish you, not after the reports I've been given about your efforts. Let's adjourn to my office, where we can have a proper conversation."

We followed him in. He must've been pretending to be surprised by Ginger and Joey, because instead of the usual three chairs in front of his desk, there were five.

Tanner didn't tip back when he sat down.

"The servants said you were covered in blood. I'm sorry for what you had to go through."

I looked at the others. Joey was accepting the apologies by nodding, Ginger was looking down at Kingsman–pretending she didn't need to hear it–, Fitz was looking down at his hands, and Tanner was preparing to tip back in his chair.

"Tanner, Kennedy, you are hereby fully pardoned. Piper–"

"His name is Fitz," Ginger and I corrected at the same time.

"My apologies, I suppose I forgot to ask. Fitz, the King hasn't determined what to do with you."

Fitz nodded, but I shook my head.

"He saved us. He stopped the army," I said.

Kingsman looked at me, "You seem to have lost your quick wit. I know he saved you, but the army was one he created in the first place."

"Daemon John was the real problem though," I said, trying to whip my thoughts into shape. They refused to be herded, and I worried that maybe I really had lost my wit.

"Isn't that the case," Kingsman sighed, "I've given you the good news. Now for the bad. Befreiung der Verdammten is indeed tied to Daemon John, and he has put an in an order for the King's head."

I wasn't shocked. Something in my head said, "the cultists faith is bought, because the gemstones they believe will revive them are only supplied by the leader. If the leader threatens to withhold them they'd do anything, but it probably wouldn't even come to that. Their gratitude goes beyond reason, and they do not fear death because they believe they'll come back."

I repeated the words aloud and Kingsman's head listed to the side, "You've said that exact thing before."

I shrugged, but thought to myself that it was a different girl who'd said those things before. That Kennedy had chosen to stop an army to become a legend, and to appease her friend. This

Kennedy knew better.

Still, I wasn't a completely different person. I knew I was clever. I never went to school, but I was smart. I designed traps, I understood concepts easily, and I could beat anyone at a game of Tricks.

"If I tell you how to stop Befreiung der Verdammten," I started, "can you do three things for me?"

That piqued everyone's interest.

Kingsman leaned forward, "The best researchers in the kingdom are studying this problem. Do you think you can do better than them?"

"I know I can, and that's why I have my first request. You mentioned school to me before. I want to go to one. A good one. My second ask is that Fitz is granted a full pardon.."

Kingsman nodded, "If your solution is effective you can have all of that."

"The cultists only serve with such fervent devotion because that's how they believe they earn eternal life, and because they aren't afraid of death when that life is guaranteed," I spoke in a familiar cadence, and found a spring of happiness when I realized I hadn't entirely lost my wit, "I have three ideas. The first would be to create copycat enchantments out of amethyst."

Kingsman shook his head, "People have tried before. Enchanters cannot enchant amethyst, which is why Daemon John used it. Only witches can attach magicks to the gem. There are nearly no witches who can create high quality enchantments that could be sold."

I thought of Ginger's mom, and met Ginger's eye, "I know one who'd make you hundreds of well crafted spells for a six legged salamander."

Kingsman nodded, "That could probably be arranged."

"Now for my other two ideas. I was gifted a collection of gemstones from a higher up member of the cult. These include enchantments like greatness, loved, power, and all kinds of even rarer ones, like denial. I'm sure the young and poor cultists, the ones who'd attack the King for the gemstones Daemon offered, would turn on Daemon and bring his head to you for such a bounty."

"That idea has class," Kingsman sounded genuinely interested.

"For my third idea you'd need a coalition of necromancers. You could sell tokens that guaranteed a person's revival by necromancer. Then fewer people would turn to Befreiung der Verdammten for life. Not to mention, you'd have adult necromancers on hand to handle things instead of hiring me for everything. I'm sure there are others."

Kingsman took a sip from his mug, "my researchers had most of the same pieces as you. They suggested we create gemstones and flood the market, but they didn't know a witch who'd do it for a six legged salamander. They suggested we put a bounty on Daemon's head, but they didn't suggest making his own cult turn against him. As for the third, that's a unique idea, but it has potential."

Tanner grinned, "That's why you sent us to stop the army,

we're smarter than you adults give us credit for."

When Kingsman only stared off into space, I cleared my throat.

Kingsman smiled and I thought it might be the first genuine smile I'd seen—before he'd smiled out of obligation or because it was the social norm—this time when he smiled he seemed truly happy.

"I'm no genie, but just this once, I think I can make your wishes happen. You did fix my back after all. I find I'm more grateful for it everyday," His eyes glittered when he smiled, "Now what was your third wish?"

"Make us legends."

Since it was Kingsman we were dealing with, he of course did as he'd promised, but he'd also done it in the most difficult way possible.

He hired us to kill Daemon John, and promised us the bounty his researchers had suggested.

Word of his treasonous actions had been spread far and wide already, so the easiest way to become legends would be to bring him in ourselves. Besides, Kingsman promised, we'd be paid well enough to spend the rest of our lives relaxing—knowing us, that would never happen, but also knowing us, it was a prospect we couldn't turn down.

No one was sure where Daemon was but Joey knew exactly where to begin our search. He said there were many among the aristocracy that had philosophies or beliefs similar to Befreiung der Verdammten. It made sense that Daemon would seek shelter

226

from the nobles, since he needed to keep an eye on the King.

Lord Donnovan, a noble who'd fallen out of favor with the king, was discovered to be the one harboring Daemon. To my glee, Daemon was staying in the very summer house I'd once fallen asleep in. I knew the layout well enough that it made planning simple.

There was no doubt Daemon John would know Fitz had been pardoned, so he'd likely have his ears stuffed. Still, we would use Fitz to draw away the guards, then Tanner and I would swim in through one of the upper windows, using one of Ginger's matter confusion potions.

Hopefully we'd surprise Daemon John, and we had sleep potions designed for olfactory attack just in case. After last time he may even have something prepared to keep him safe from that, but that's why I made crossbow bolts that split into nets when they were launched. We could either knock Daemon John out, or trap him in a net and haul him out the front.

Once the plan was solidified the only thing to do was execute it. Joey offered one of his family's steam wagons, and we took it for a portion of the drive. The wagon was too loud to bring right up to the summer home, so the five of us hopped out and continued on foot.

We'd ditched our bright costumes for more practical dark cloaks. Fitz started playing nearly immediately, in case of sentries. He didn't play any songs I knew, instead he let the notes flow together in one long line, unspooling like a line of wind around the oaks.

We reached the lawn, and paused before leaving the treeline. Across the soft grass the manor stretched toward the moon. A cobbled drive circled a fountain, and an elegant veranda stood out from the structure.

"Let's move forward, slowly. The upper lights are out, so Daemon and Donnovan are likely asleep. The servants are still cleaning the lower floors, and Fitz can draw them out," Joey said.

We all nodded. Ginger passed Tanner and I small yellow vials, and we both tipped our heads back and drank.

Tanner tried to float through the air immediately, but I waited until I was hit by the sensation of being dunked. Then I started to paddle through the air. Neither Tanner nor I were particularly graceful swimmers, but we made it to the second floor without a hitch. We perched on the window sills until the servants spilled from the front doors and out onto the cobbled road. Joey gave the signal, telling us Daemon hadn't joined them out on the lawn.

We splashed one of Ginger's specialty acids on the window, and the glass melted down the frames and dripped in wax-like streams down the wall.

Tanner and I floated through the window just before the potion wore off. We landed lightly on the floorboards of the hallway. Tanner led the way, raising his crossbow to shoulder height as he crept forward.

We tried to avoid making too much noise, but knew that if Daemon couldn't hear the flute, he probably wouldn't hear us either.

There was a great amount less dust than the previous time

I'd stayed there, but other than that it was just as I remembered. We'd assumed Daemon would be in one of the nicer rooms on the upper floors, because he seemed like someone to enjoy luxury.

Tanner picked the first lock, his fingers a blur of indecipherable motion. The lock clicked softly, and he turned the doorknob slowly. We both readied ourselves for a sudden attack, and Tanner kicked open the door.

No traps went off. The room was empty.

We snuck to the next door and repeated the process. No traps went off when we opened the door, but it wasn't empty. Lord Donnovan didn't rouse when we stepped into the room, but we broke one of the sleep potions over his bed anyway.

"He's in this next one, I can feel it," Tanner muttered, picking the lock on the third door.

We both stood to the side of the door, and Tanner kicked it in. It was lucky we were prepared, because there was an immediate commotion in the doorway.

A net, not unlike the ones I'd built for our crossbows, exploded out from the doorway, followed closely by a hail of arrows.

Once they were all quivering in the wall opposite, we entered the room. Tanner held his crossbow, and I had the sleep potion.

Daemon John was scrambling out of his bed, clumps of cotton sticking from his ears. He was reaching for something on the nightstand, but he never got the chance.

The net and potion burst at the same time, and Daemon John was sent reeling as his eyes rolled up into his skull.

Daemon was knocked out as easily as any other man had been. The ingenious trap maker's traps had failed him.

We both grabbed corners of the net, and started dragging Daemon outside, until we remembered there was an easier–and less painful–way of getting him out there. I called through the melted window to have the servants bring him out with us.

Fitz gestured, and a group of them came inside and helped us gather him. What's more, they helped us carry him all the way back to the steam powered trolley,

Tanner got carried too, and was extremely proud of himself for it.

We delivered Daemon John to the palace gates, and Kingsman delivered on his promise. We became legends.

Life settled back into it's regular rhythms, and we lived life as usual.

Except it wasn't really as usual. Joey had decided to apprentice to one of Kingsman's researchers, and helped create new policy on necromancy and chartered the Necromancy Guild. Ginger created more unique potions, and also learned a fair few spells. We celebrated Fitz's birthday whenever the urge hit us– sometimes he'd have ten birthdays a year. Tanner spent less time robbing houses, and more at the theater, and he landed a major role in a summer play. I discovered that I could revive plants as well as creatures, and I kept our house covered in blooming flowers no matter the season.

Before any of that, Joey's parents hosted a party to celebrate...who knows what they were celebrating, but we were all invited. Tanner's mother sent him with a basketful of bread as hard as rock, and we made it a game, seeing who could eat it the fastest. Tanner and I finally wrestled, and I beat him—the luck charm clutched in my palm.

Our story was outlandish, but the bards told it well. They alway started with something like this, "They weren't the best heroes in the kingdom, probably not even the best in the capital, but no one could say they weren't determined. They did their jobs with reckless abandon, so lean in close and listen, as I tell the story of how five teenagers saved the world as we know it."

Acknowledgements

I would like to thank everyone who helped me through this project, but listing their names would be awfully dull. Instead I will list their epithets. Thank you to clever, helpful, conspiratorial, kind, supportive, and avid for their help with the editing. This next group will be listed by (likely) unappreciated nicknames; I'd like to thank skywalker, crimped updo, alex, and orange for serving as inspiration. Lastly, I'd like to thank my mentor in this project who helped it all come together, my family for reminding me of how famous I'm going to be, my science teacher for the fish dissections that allowed me to experience rigor mortis, and my childhood self for reading so many inspirational novels.

I'd also like to thank the trees I stared at when I couldn't think of what to say next, and my sketchbook–in which I documented every creative idea for a death.

Congratulations! You made it to the end of the book! What's more, you're one of the curious souls who found this last page and decided to read it. I commend you for your dedication, although there's no accounting for taste. You could be doing something much cooler, like killing a dragon, or saving the kingdom (now that you know how).

To summarize, I'm a teenage author, writing novels for other teenagers. This first novel was written and published as a senior project.

The family dog's name is Prim, and she follows me around and begs for food I only sometimes give her. The cat's name is Yang (there was a Yin...once) and he's the sweetest cat that's ever existed. There are also a few dozen houseplants, but they never respond when I call them. If you're interested, a few of their unofficial names are Donny, Laffy, Jin, and Taft. As for other interesting author notes, I love dark chocolate, ultimate frisbee, and most kinds of music. If you were curious, the main genre I listened to while I wrote this novel was grunge punk.

Once again, I'd like to congratulate you on making it this far, and to sincerely thank you for reading this book. It's the fulfillment of a childhood dream, and if there's one thing that I want you to know about me, it's that I won't give up on my dreams. (Neither should you.)